# WILD JEWEL

## TYSON WILD BOOK THIRTY SEVEN

### TRIPP ELLIS

D1212052

TRIPP ELLIS

# CONTENTS

# 1

---

"**D**eputy Wild, my name is Jean-Claude Juneau," the man said with a slight French accent.

The call had buzzed my phone on an encrypted messaging app. I didn't really have time to talk, and I didn't usually answer unrecognized numbers. But, given the current situation, I thought the call could have been pertaining to another urgent matter.

The man continued, "I have a pressing security concern, and from what I understand, you are the man to talk to."

"I'm en route to a crime scene at the moment," I said. "Can I call you back?"

"Certainly. While my concern is not urgent, it is time-sensitive."

"Understood. I will get back with you as soon as I can."

I ended the call and slipped the phone back into my pocket.

The engine howled as we zipped across the island in JD's lava orange convertible Porsche. The cool night air swirled around, and the stars flickered above. The wind tousled JD's long blond hair. He wore his typical uniform of a Hawaiian shirt, cargo shorts, and checkered Vans. Music pumped through the speakers filling the cabin with '80s rock. The full moon hung in the sky, casting a glow over the island, bringing out the crazies.

It had done its job tonight.

Red and blue lights flickered as we pulled onto the scene a block away from Oyster Avenue. Emergency personnel swarmed the area, and deputies managed the crowd. Several ambulances were on hand, lights flashing. A crowd of mildly inebriated spectators looked on in horror. The tragic event at the Frisky Kitty would haunt the island for some time to come.

The sounds of revelry from Oyster Avenue filtered down the block. Music from live bands and booming bass from dance clubs mixed with the smell of grilled food, beer, and whiskey.

The neon signage of *Frisky Kitty* bathed the sidewalk in tones of teal and pink.

We pushed past the deputies and came to the first casualty.

A big barrel-chested guy lay slumped against the wall by the entrance. Two cavernous wounds in his chest oozed crimson. Blood had soaked his shirt and pooled around his lifeless body.

Brenda, the medical examiner, hovered over the corpse, examining the remains.

Dietrich snapped crime scene photos, and camera flashes bounced off the wall and sidewalk.

"Two to the chest," Brenda said as I stepped to her. Pink nitrile gloves protected her hands and minimized contamination. "Small caliber. Probably 9mm."

"How many more are there?" I asked.

"Step inside and find out," she said in a grim voice.

I didn't want to find out.

From what Sheriff Daniels had told me, I knew it would be bad.

We pushed inside. A girl behind the register lay on the floor behind the counter. Bullet wounds riddled her chest. She was young and pretty—mid-20s, sandy brown hair.

My face tensed, and a sickening feeling twisted in my gut. This was just the beginning of the carnage.

Forensic investigators swarmed about. The house lights were up, and the club had been emptied of patrons. Only first responders and a few staff members were inside.

The *Frisky Kitty* was a members-only swingers' club. Single ladies and couples were welcome any night of the week. Single men were allowed Wednesday through Friday. The membership fee was $200 a month, plus a nightly cover charge. It was BYOB, but three bars served setups, so the club skated all those pesky laws that apply to venues that serve.

There was a central dance floor, and cozy booths surrounded the perimeter. There were plenty of couches, chairs, and places to lounge. Two main bars on either side of the dance floor provided mixables. Private *playrooms* in the back, where nudity was encouraged, were home to the real action.

Frisky, slippery, naughty action.

You could participate or watch. A small bar in the back helped quench the thirst of those who worked up a sweat.

With Valentine's Day drawing near, I couldn't help but think this was a crime of passion. Jealousy turned to rage. Watching your wife get on her knees for some random guy is not everyone's cup of tea.

There were pools of blood and speckles of spatter throughout the club. Brass shell casings littered the floor, along with an empty 30 round magazine.

I knelt down and examined the spent brass—.223, 55-grain full metal jackets.

The place had an odd mixture of smells—whiskey, the faint smell of sex masked by the remnants of perfume and cologne, all subdued by the scent of gunpowder and blood.

Several bodies lay on the ground to the left of the dance floor near the main bar, close to the high-top tables. Three were grouped together with another victim close to a neighboring table.

Sheriff Daniels hovered near the bodies with a couple of forensic investigators. He gave me a look as we approached, utter disgust on his face. His jaw was tight, and his eyes narrow.

"What happened?" I asked.

"Some jackass stormed in here and started putting holes in people. That's what happened."

"I can see that. Any idea why?"

"Why is the sky blue?"

"You think these targets were random or intentional?"

The sheriff shrugged. "I don't pretend to know anything anymore. The world just doesn't make sense to me. We've got six dead and another half dozen wounded that are en route to the hospital."

"Any security footage?" I asked.

"This isn't the kind of place that people like to be photographed entering and exiting." Daniels pointed to a young blonde standing nearby.

She looked frazzled. Understandably so.

"She's a waitress here," Daniels continued. "Described the shooter as 5'10", average build, wearing a ski mask. Her name is Tanya."

I stepped to her, flashed my badge, and made introductions. "Can you tell me exactly what you saw?"

# 2

———

Tanya's voice quivered, and her body trembled. Her eyes were round like the full moon. "I heard two pops. Then two more. I wasn't sure what was happening at first. I thought maybe it was a car backfiring on the street or something. Then this guy stormed in. He holstered his pistol, marched across the dance floor, and shouldered an assault rifle. He shot those three people," she said, pointing to the trio on the floor by the high-top table. "And then he shot that girl." She pointed again to a nearby victim. "He was all business. He turned around and headed for the door. There was a guy in a booth by the exit. He was carrying. He pulled out a pistol and shot at the shooter. They exchanged fire. The guy got hit, and the shooter rushed out. They rushed the guy to the hospital. I hope he's okay."

"These three victims here," I said, pointing. "Have you ever seen them before?"

She nodded. "Yeah, they're regulars."

"What about the other girl?"

"I've seen her in here a few times."

"They have any trouble in here before?"

She shook her head. "Not that I know of. Most people that come in here are pretty laid back. I mean, it gets a little wild in the playrooms. Every now and then, somebody freaks out. They're not really ready for what goes on. They *think* they're ready. The idea of it seems interesting. But when they get down to it, this lifestyle is a different ballgame."

"Has anybody made any threats against the establishment?" I asked.

"You probably need to talk to my manager, Larry."

She waved over a guy in his mid-30s. He was 6'1", brown hair, brown eyes, average build. We shook hands, and I asked him about previous threats.

"You know, we get our fair share of hate. Not everybody agrees with what goes on here, and I understand that. But hey, it's a free country. Everyone here is an adult. They can do what they want to do." He paused. "If you want a list of suspects, just scroll through the comments on our social media pages. That's a treasure trove. If I had a nickel for every time somebody said they wanted me to burn in hell."

Brenda entered the club and started to examine the trio while Dietrich snapped photos of blood splatter and shell casings.

Brenda fished a driver's license from a victim's purse. The woman was among the trio near the high-top table. "Dawn Young. 36."

Dawn was a pretty blonde with hair that hung just past her shoulders. 5'4", blue eyes, and a great figure wrapped in a slinky black cocktail dress with a deep V-neck. Her empty, lifeless eyes stared at the ceiling.

According to their IDs, her two companions were Crosby Gallagher and Brooke Adams.

Crosby was a young, good-looking guy with a square jaw lined with stubble, dark brown hair, brooding brown eyes, and an athletic build. The kind of guy you'd see on the cover of men's magazines. At 24, he looked like he had everything going for him until this evening.

Brooke Adams rounded out the trio. She was a gorgeous young brunette—23, aqua eyes, and a petite figure. Brooke wore an eye-catching red dress that hugged her curves like a Formula One race car.

The trio was dressed to the nines. Crosby wore a DiFiore suit and an Affini watch that cost more than my first car. The *Frisky Kitty* had a strict dress code, despite the fact that most of it ended up on the floor at some point during the night. Clothing was optional in the playrooms.

The lone girl nearby was Tara Ward. She had long, dark brown hair, brown eyes, and a svelte figure. She also wore a form-fitting, skimpy black cocktail dress.

Beautiful people gunned down in the prime of their lives.

One by one, the bodies were bagged and removed. Forensic investigators cataloged everything, and Dietrich filled flash-cards full of gruesome images.

We interviewed other witnesses and got varying accounts of the same basic story. Some said the gunman was 5'10", another said he was 6'1". Another cocktail waitress said he was 5'6". Some said he was stocky. Others said he was lean.

The trouble with eyewitness testimony is that it's often incorrect. People misremember facts. The stress of the moment can distort perception.

We wrapped up at the club. Paris Delaney was outside with her news crew, capturing footage as the bodies were rolled out on yellow gurneys, zipped in black bags. The ambitious blonde didn't miss a thing. She had sources everywhere, and I was pretty sure someone in the department was on her payroll.

As soon as I stepped outside, a camera was in my face.

"Deputy Wild, do you have any idea who the shooter is?"

"Not at this time."

"Can you give us an official body count?"

"High," I said, mildly annoyed.

JD and I made our way back to the Porsche and headed to the station. We filled out after-action reports. In the conference room, we spoke with Daniels, Denise, and several other deputies that had worked the scene.

"I want the son-of-a-bitch responsible off the street ASAP!" Daniels barked.

"What do we know about the victims?" I asked.

"Dawn Young," Denise said. "36 years old, married with two kids—14 and 16. Spouse is Greg Young. They have separate addresses listed."

"Divorced?" JD asked.

"Looks like they're in the process."

I cringed, thinking about their kids. Somebody would have to tell them their mother wasn't coming home. "Do we know if Greg Young was in the club?"

Daniels shrugged.

I exchanged a glance with JD. "We'll run down that lead."

It sounded the most promising—jealous husband finds out his wife is going to a swingers' bar with a 24-year-old hunk.

Definitely motive.

Denise gave us Dawn's info, and we headed to her apartment. She lived in a luxury complex on Inca Dove Lane. The coral-colored building was a few blocks from the beach. The units had large balconies around a central pool. Palm trees lined the grounds.

We parked in the lot and made our way to #222. I had the Department of Children and Families meet us there. It was late, almost midnight, when I knocked on the door.

# 3

The TV filtered through the door. The sounds of a superhero movie rumbled. A young boy's voice called through the door a moment later. "Who is it?"

The peephole flickered.

"Coconut County," I said, holding my badge to the peephole. "We need to talk to you about your mother."

A skinny kid with shaggy brown hair and brown eyes pulled open the door. He looked us up and down. "Are you guys really cops?"

"Yeah," I said in a grim tone.

"You don't look like cops."

I shrugged.

"What happened? She get another DUI?"

I frowned. "I'm afraid it's a little more serious than that."

The kid lifted a concerned brow.

"Are you Liam?" I asked.

He nodded.

I broke the bad news to him, and he started bawling. It wasn't long before his sister, Whitney, was at the door. Tears sprouted from their eyes. The two sobbed and consoled each other.

It was a horrible feeling to see them like this. And even if we brought the killer to justice, it wouldn't bring their mother back. Nothing would ever fill that hole. No matter what we did, this wasn't a problem we could solve.

The kids cried until their tear ducts ran dry. Eyes were puffy, and noses red and running.

"Do you know who did this?" Liam asked.

"Not yet. Where's your father?" I asked.

"He's probably at home. Does he know?"

"I'm not sure. Can you tell me what their relationship was like?"

Liam scoffed. "What relationship? Mom left him three months ago. We moved here."

"Have you seen him since?"

Liam shook his head. "No. And I don't want to. He's a dick." He paused, and a terrible thought flooded over him. "I'm not going to live with him. You can't make me."

DCS arrived, and I introduced him to Ruth Webb. "She's with the Department of Children and Families. She'll be handling your case."

"I'm 16. I can take care of myself. Mom leaves me to look after Whitney all the time. I can take care of her."

"You're 16," I repeated. "Do you have a job?"

He shook his head.

"Rent here's expensive."

"I'll find a way to pay it. I can get emancipated, can't I?"

"We can talk about this in detail later," Ruth said.

"Do you know why your mother left your father?" I asked.

"I don't know. I guess she got tired of him hitting her. Fuck that guy. You can't make me go live with him." A wave of realization washed over his face. "He didn't do this, did he?"

"Did he ever make threats?"

"All the time. She had a restraining order against him, but he still called and harassed her," Liam said.

"Does your father still live on Sandhill Court?"

Liam nodded. "I think." He pulled his phone from his pocket and dialed. It rang a few times and went to voicemail. Liam burst into tears again as he left a message, "What did you do? Mom's dead. Did you kill her?"

He shouted and cursed, then broke down into sobs as he ranted. He finally lost the ability to speak as his throat tightened with sadness. Only a dry screech emanated.

His distress spurred on Whitney, and the two melted down again.

After they recovered, I asked, "Was your mom dating anyone else?"

Liam shrugged. "I don't know. She went out drinking a lot with Jillian, but she never told me she was dating anyone."

"Who's Jillian?"

"Her best friend."

"Was she with Jillian tonight?"

"I don't think so," he sniffled. "I mean, she usually tells me where she's going."

"What did she say tonight?"

"Just that she was meeting a friend at a bar and not to wait up."

"You happen to have Jillian's contact information?"

He nodded. "If I couldn't get hold of mom, I could always call Jillian."

He gave me Jillian's number, and I gave him my card. I told him to call me if he needed anything. Ruth took over, and we left to find Greg Young.

That horrible feeling twisted in my stomach as we left. I felt so bad for those kids.

"My money's on the husband," JD said as we stepped onto the elevator.

We rode it down, pushed out of the lobby and into the parking lot. We climbed into the Porsche and zipped over to the house at Sandhill Court.

It was a nice two-story with a picket fence and a yard full of palm trees. A white Jeep sat in the driveway. There was a brick shoulder for parking before the picket fence.

We hopped out of the Porsche, pushed through the gate, and made our way to the front porch. With my palm on my pistol grip, I put a heavy fist against the mahogany door.

After no response, I banged my fist again. "Coconut County! Open up."

There were a few lights on the house.

We waited a moment, then started nosing around the shrubs, peering through windows. It didn't take long for me to catch a glimpse of Greg through a bay window. He was sitting on a couch in the living room. At first glance, he looked asleep.

The TV flickered, casting a glow.

The wall behind the couch was splattered with crimson.

Greg wasn't asleep, and that crimson splatter wasn't modern art.

I rushed back to the front door and checked the handle. It was locked. I kicked the hell out of the door. It took a few tries, but it finally splintered the jam and swung open. We advanced through the foyer, into the living room, and took in the gruesome sight.

# 4

———

"Looks open and shut," Daniels said, observing Greg's remains.

Dietrich snapped photos, and Brenda hovered over the body. Deputies milled about, and a crowd of curious neighbors gathered outside. The flickering red and blue lights were hard to ignore, even at this time of night.

An AR 15 rested on the couch beside Greg. He had a 9mm in his hand. He had presumably stuck the pistol in his mouth and pulled the trigger. His hand had fallen into his lap, the weapon still loosely in it.

The tinny metallic scent of blood filled the air, and a fly buzzed around the corpse. Greg didn't look too bad from the front, but the back of his skull had seen better days.

"This guy goes into a rage when he finds out his wife is diddling everybody but him, and he shoots up the club for revenge," Daniels speculated.

"I'm not so sure about that," Brenda said.

"Sure about what?"

"The open and shut part."

Daniels stifled a groan.

"For a guy that blew his brains out, there's no blood splatter on his hand," Brenda said.

We all leaned in close and hovered over the weapon.

"Son-of-a-bitch," Daniels grumbled, unable to deny the obvious.

"Also, the angle of trajectory doesn't match. When people stick a gun in their mouth, the weapon usually angles upward. This exit wound is level."

"Maybe he held the weapon at an awkward angle," Daniels said, hoping this wouldn't be a complicated case. He knew it was wishful thinking.

"Possible. But the lack of blood spatter is concerning."

"Somebody went to an awful lot of trouble to frame this guy," I said.

"It would have to be somebody who knew they were having marital trouble," JD added.

"Start digging into Dawn Young's background," Daniels said. "Find out who would want her dead, besides her husband."

"Maybe the husband was the target," JD suggested.

"Seems a bit elaborate, but I wouldn't rule anything out at this point."

"Are there any signs of forced entry?" I asked.

"Only the door you kicked down," Daniels muttered.

"I haven't seen any broken windows," a forensic investigator said. "Locks don't look tampered with."

"There's something else," Brenda said. "I can't say with absolute certainty, but the body temperature suggests that he was killed at least an hour before the shootings at the club."

"So, the real killer comes here, shoots Greg with his own weapon. Takes his AR 15 to the club, unleashes fury, then comes back here and deposits the weapons," I postulated.

"That sounds about right," Brenda said.

"I don't think you're gonna find anything, but dust the doorknobs and surfaces for prints," I said. "The person who did this is definitely a planner. This wasn't spur of the moment. It was cold and calculated."

Paris and her crew were on the scene when we stepped outside. She marched my way, and the camera followed. "Deputy Wild, is this connected to the Frisky Kitty Massacre?"

"I can't comment at this time."

"Is it true that Greg Young took his own life?"

The cameras outside had a clear view of the carnage, zooming in through the window.

"Again, no comment."

"Was he the shooter?"

I gave her an annoyed look and marched to the crowd of neighbors. "Anybody see anything?"

They all shook their heads.

"Any visitors come and go?"

They all exchanged blank glances and shrugged.

"Anybody got a video doorbell with an angle on this house?"

More blank faces.

We knocked on neighbors' doors, looking for anyone with a video doorbell. Unfortunately, we couldn't find any security footage of Greg's house.

After we wrapped up at the scene, we headed to the station and filled out more reports. By that time, I was ready to call it a night.

JD dropped me off at the marina, and I hustled down the dock to the *Avventura*. It was calm and peaceful at this hour. A gentle breeze swirled around, and the boats swayed in their slips. The moon glimmered the water. And at least one person was getting some late-night action. Moans of ecstasy drifted in the air, and a 32' sailboat had a little extra sway.

Buddy greeted me as I slid open the glass door to the salon of the superyacht. The little Jack Russell was eager to stretch his legs. I leashed him up and took him out for a late-night stroll, then settled in for the night.

I'd forgotten all about Jean-Claude, but he reminded me with an early morning phone call. My cell buzzed on the nightstand as the morning sun sneaked in through the cracks.

I grabbed the phone, swiped the screen, and tried not to sound asleep.

"Good morning, Deputy Wild. I hate to bother you so early, but as I mentioned yesterday, this is a time-sensitive matter. I need to know if I can count on your assistance."

"My apologies," I said in a scratchy tone. "There was a terrible situation last night that went on until the wee hours of the morning."

"I assume you're referring to the mass shooting. A horrific tragedy. It's all over the national news."

"What can I do for you?"

"Do you have time for a video conference? I'd like to speak face-to-face."

"Sure. Can you give me 15 minutes?"

"Certainly. As you may notice, I prefer to use only encrypted communications."

"I'll call you back on this app momentarily."

"I await your call."

I disconnected, pulled myself out of bed, and made my way down to the galley for a bowl of cereal. I took a shower, got dressed, then used my laptop to connect via the encrypted messaging app.

## 5

J ean-Claude was in his 50s with short curly brown hair that was graying on the sides, giving him a distinguished quality. He had sharp, angular features and a narrow face. He had slim blue eyes and the requisite amount of wrinkles for a man of his age. He looked impeccably dressed and carried himself as a man with extreme confidence and means. He was a handsome man, and I was sure he did well with the ladies. The accent gave him an unfair competitive advantage.

"Thank you for speaking with me. I will get straight down to business," Jean-Claude said. "Are you familiar with the Jewels of Aphrodite?"

"I am not."

"Three priceless rubies. Legend has it, they were given to the goddess Aphrodite by Ares as a token of his love. Forged in the heavens, unrivaled in their perfection, the gems captured the goddess's heart. But a cunning thief managed to steal them from Mount Olympus, drawing the ire of Aphrodite. The gems were quickly sold to three different buyers, each believing the stones possessed magical qualities. Aphrodite cursed the stones and all those who possess them, except for the pure of heart. It is said that the person who reunites all three stones and returns them to Olympus will control the power contained within them. Of course, this is all myth and legend, but that kind of lore does wondrous things for a gem's value. "

"And what power is contained within the stones?" I asked, my curiosity piqued.

"The power of love, of course. The ability to make anyone fall in love with the bearer of the stones."

"Do you believe the legend?"

Jean-Claude smiled. "Of course not. But there are those who do. And they will do anything to acquire the gems. No cost is too great, no sacrifice too much."

"Despite the curse?"

"As I said, no sacrifice is too great. Besides, most people think they are pure of heart, don't they?"

"All for love?"

"Isn't that all there really is, Deputy? Money, status, power… it's all a means to attract the things you desire, isn't it?"

"I'm not sure I'd be interested in someone who was only attracted to me because of my wealth, power, or status."

Jean-Claude smiled again. "I agree. Love should be pure and unadulterated." He paused. "That is the great paradox of wealth. The more you acquire, the more difficult it becomes to trust the motives of those around you. I find it ironic that most men try to woo women with displays of wealth and status, then they are shocked to learn the person they attracted is only interested in their finances."

"Pretend to be poor."

"Says the man speaking to me from a superyacht."

He'd obviously done a little homework on me. "Let me guess, you're either in possession of a stone, or you want to acquire all three?"

Jean-Claude grinned. "You're perceptive, Deputy Wild. You have a keen sense and unwavering loyalty."

"Is that what they tell you about me?"

"I don't do business with anyone I haven't thoroughly vetted. And to your question, yes, I own one of the stones." He displayed a picture on the screen of a sparkling red ruby with a classic round cut.

Flawless.

"I'm loaning it to the museum in Coconut Key. The delightful curator is extremely persuasive. And she's right. A gem of such perfection and beauty needs to be seen and experienced by all. Not hoarded away, kept in a vault where it can't be enjoyed."

"And you need me to ensure its safety."

"As I said, Deputy. You're very perceptive."

"I'm sure you have private security staff."

"I do, and they are more than qualified. But I'm a man who likes to measure twice and cut once. I plan for every conceivable contingency. And I can't overstate the desirability of this stone."

He sent an image to my computer screen of a gruff man with a long face and narrow lips. He had a perpetual scowl on his face. His long nose had been flattened a few times by fists, and his head was cue ball slick. The man was nearing 60, and his steely eyes had seen a lot of horrors. This was a man who had ice water in his veins.

"Do you recognize this man?"

"I can't say I have had the pleasure of making his acquaintance."

"Consider yourself lucky. And hopefully, you will never cross paths with him. His name is Anatoly Vetrov—a Russian gangster known to deal in high-end gems. He's collected two of the stones already, and he seeks to possess the third. Of course, he's reached out to me and made ridiculous lowball offers, stating in no uncertain terms that should I fail to comply, I will suffer the consequences." Jean-Claude took a breath. "I am not a man to be intimidated, but Anatoly's threats do carry weight."

"You think he's going to make a move on the stone?"

"I can guarantee it. He won't likely do it himself. He'll use hired guns. Pros. My sources tell me he's put an offer out and received a few bids. I know who's taken his offer." Jean-Claude paused. "Are you interested in learning more?"

---

## 6

Jean-Claude sent a photo of a man in his late 30s. He had chiseled features, suspicious blue eyes, and brown hair with bangs that fell to his brow. He looked both sophisticated and slimy at the same time.

"That's Charles Le Grand. International jewel thief. Notorious in Europe. Suspected in over a dozen high-profile cases, but the authorities have never been able to make anything stick."

Jean-Claude sent another image. This one certainly got my attention.

The young brunette in the photo was nothing short of mesmerizing and enigmatic. Her long raven hair dangled well past her shoulders, obscuring most of her face. Her eyes were covered by sunglasses, and a stylish black Trilby hat sat at an angle atop her head. Her striking curves begged a second glance. The sultry vixen inspired naughty fantasies.

"That's the only photo I have of Lily Lovelace. She has multiple aliases and frequently changes her appearance. She goes from blonde to brunette to redhead at the drop of a dime. A chameleon. As you can see, she's quite easy on the eyes, and her charms have duped more than a few wealthy men. Fortunes have been lost. Millions absconded with. If you should encounter her, I would urge you to use caution and let your logical brain prevail. She's cunning and deadly."

"She looks... dangerous," I said.

"I'm well aware of your proclivities, Deputy Wild. She may attempt to exploit that weakness. She can be rather enthralling."

"I'll keep that in mind."

"I expect both to make an attempt at some point."

"Do you have any idea when and where?"

"I would suspect during transit. I'm personally bringing the jewel from my home in New York to Coconut Key."

"I have my hands full now with this recent incident," I said.

"I will only require your services once I arrive in Coconut Key. I've made arrangements for the New York segment of the journey."

"What about the museum?"

"I've coordinated with the curator, and I'm satisfied with their arrangements. Though, I would like you to make an evaluation and threat assessment."

"So, you want me to handle transport to and from the museum here in Coconut Key?"

"Yes, I would. I'm more than happy to compensate you for your time."

I contemplated the assignment. The last thing I needed was to take on another case, but it had me intrigued. One way or another, I was sure my involvement was inevitable. I spoke with confidence, "We can get your jewel to the museum without incident."

Jean-Claude grinned again. "Excellent. I'll be in touch with further details. I have a plan for your segment of the journey, which I will share with you soon. Please maintain operational security."

"I work with a partner, Jack Donovan. I trust him with my life."

"I'm aware of your association with Mr. Donovan. I defer to your judgment as to who you feel is secure and who is not." He paused. "Until we speak again."

Jean-Claude ended the call, and I dialed JD. I filled him in on the situation, and he swung by the marina to pick me up.

I grabbed two boxes of Valentine's Day chocolate and cards that I had picked up the day before. I met JD in the parking lot. He pulled around by the dock and waited with the top down.

"How sweet," he teased. "Are those for me?"

I frowned at him. "No, stupid."

I tossed a box and a card onto the seat then hustled into *Diver Down.* Teagan's eyes brightened behind the bar when she saw me.

"Oooh, for moi?"

"A little token of my appreciation for everything you do around here. Happy early Valentine's Day."

"Are you trying to fatten me up?"

"I don't think you have anything to worry about." Teagan had an amazing figure. And she wasn't shy about showing it off with her skimpy bikini top and tight shorts, her bare midriff flat as a board.

"Should I open the card now?"

"You can if you want?"

Her nails dug into the envelope and tore it open. She pulled out the card, and her eyes misted as she read it. She rushed around the bar and gave me a hug, squeezing tight.

She had a nice squeeze. I could stay like this for as long as she wanted, her warm body against mine.

"I feel the same way about you. You're the best boss a girl could have."

"Get your hands off my girl, Sonny," Harlan shouted from the end of the bar.

Teagan lifted up and kissed my cheek. She put a hand on my heart for a moment then pushed away, returning to the bar. "I'm nobody's girl, Harlan. Not yet, anyway."

She gave me a flirty glance before I darted out of the bar and hopped into the Porsche.

Jack's phone buzzed with a call as we pulled out of the lot. He took the call and held the phone to his ear. His eyes lit up, and a wide smile tugged his lips. "Fantastic!"

I couldn't hear the caller over the roar of the engine.

"Can you deliver it to the marina?" JD asked. He listened intently. "That's fine. If we're not here, just leave it with Teagan behind the bar. I'll send the payment. I can't wait to see it."

He ended the call and slipped the phone back into his pocket.

I gave him a curious look, but he didn't say anything. He just maintained that devilish grin.

"What was that all about?"

"You'll see."

I continued to stare at him, my eyes trying to pull out the secret.

"Just a little side project I've been working on. You're gonna freak the hell out when you see it."

"I'm gonna freak out *good* or I'm gonna freak out *bad*?"

"Oh, this is good. This is real good."

I left it at that and figured all would be revealed soon enough.

We stopped at the station, and I delivered the box of choco-lates and a card to Denise.

She lifted a curious eyebrow as I set it on her desk. "And just how many of these are you giving out?"

She knew me well.

I raised my hands innocently. "Only two. I swear."

"That seems like a low number for you."

"I'm just giving them to the special people in my life."

"I didn't get a box of chocolates," JD said.

I scowled at him.

"Who else did you give one to?" Denise asked.

"Teagan."

She pondered it for a moment. "Okay. I like Teagan. She's cute. But you have to help me eat this. You really can't expect me to eat this whole box by myself. I mean, I could, but I shouldn't."

I chuckled. "Are you going to open the card?"

"Is it mushy? Am I going to cry?"

I shrugged. "Maybe."

"I'll read it later. I'm not crying here."

I laughed.

Denise looked at JD. "Don't you have any chocolates for me?"

Jack stuttered. "I, uh, still have time."

"You better get on that, Mister," she teased.

He gave her a mock salute, and we left the station.

We headed over to Jillian Loller's apartment. She lived in the same building as Dawn Young but on the opposite side of the pool in unit #412.

I banged on the door and shouted, "Coconut County."

Jillian opened a moment later with a distressed face. She was a cute redhead in her mid 30s with tawny eyes and creamy skin. "It's just terrible," she said as her eyes started to mist. "I still can't believe it happened. Greg did this, no doubt in my mind."

"I'm not so sure about that."

Her brow crinkled. "It's pretty obvious if you ask me. I just wish he would have shot himself before taking everyone else out."

"We believe that somebody else killed Greg before the shooting at the Frisky Kitty."

Her brow lifted with astonishment.

I gave her limited details. "Can you think of anybody else who may have wanted to harm Dawn?"

Jillian thought for a moment. "No. She was so sweet. Too nice. Sometimes she let people take advantage of her. But I was proud of her when she left Greg. It took a lot of guts."

"Tell me about her relationship with Crosby."

"I guess she'd been dating him for a couple weeks. We met him out at a bar one night. He was incredibly good-looking," she said with a primal growl. "And Dawn needed to have a little fun. He introduced her to swinging, and I think she was open to trying new things. The last thing she needed was to settle down right away. I told her to go for broke, sow all those wild oats."

"What about Brooke Adams?"

"That's another victim, right? I don't know her. She must have been somebody they met at the club."

"Have you ever been to the Frisky Kitty?"

"It's not my scene." Her eyes filled, and her face crinkled with confusion. "Why would somebody try to frame Greg?"

"That's what we're trying to figure out."

"It's just so senseless."

"What about her job? Did Dawn have any issues with anybody at work?"

## 7

"**I** don't think so," Jillian said. "That's how we met. At the hospital. She was a cardiology tech. I'm in radiology."

I dug into my pocket and gave her my card. "If you can think of anything that might be helpful, please get in touch."

"I will."

We left and headed down to the lobby. Daniels called as we made our way through the parking lot. "Not shocking, but the fingerprints on the shell casings were all a match for Greg Young. Same with the print found on the magazine left at the scene. I think our killer made sure we'd trace it back to Greg." He sighed. "You making any headway?"

"Not really."

"You might find this interesting. Crosby Gallagher was the Chief of Staff for City Commissioner Dario Johnson. You might want to have a word with him. See if he knows anything. Could be politically motivated. Also, Erickson and

Faulkner talked to Gallagher's parents. They live on the island. They mentioned Crosby had an on-again off-again girlfriend named Heather Ingle. I'll send you her contact information. They described their relationship as extremely tumultuous."

"She might be worth looking into."

"We're assuming that the killer was a man, but you never know."

I ended the call as we reached the Porsche. Daniels texted me the contact information, and we zipped across the island toward City Hall. I dialed Crosby Gallagher's parents' number and spoke with his mother, Daisy. I introduced myself and told her I had a few follow-up questions. "Can you tell me a little bit about Heather Ingle and her relationship with Crosby? The sheriff gave me a brief overview."

"I like Heather. She's a sweet girl, but she was not the one for Crosby. She was too much drama. One week, they were madly in love. The next, they were fighting like cats and dogs. And when she got mad, she got *mad*. That girl was o to 60 in a split second." She sighed. "But Crosby seemed to be excited by that. And who could blame him? She's a gorgeous girl."

"They ever get violent?"

"Crosby would never lay a hand on a woman," she said, almost offended.

"Did she ever get violent with him?"

"She'd slap and punch on occasion. That girl has fire in her eyes." Daisy paused. "You don't think she had something to do with this, do you?"

"At this point, we're not ruling anything out."

"All the news reports are stating that a male gunman entered the club and..." She couldn't finish the sentence.

"Eyewitnesses can be inaccurate at times. We're keeping all possibilities in mind."

Daisy sniffled, grabbed a tissue, and blew her nose. "Excuse me. It comes in waves."

"I understand. Can you think of anyone else who may have had a vendetta against Crosby?"

"No one comes to mind. He was a really easy-going guy. Lots of friends. Outgoing. Charming. Maybe a little too outgoing. I didn't necessarily approve of some of his lifestyle choices. I can't help but think this could have all been avoided had he never set foot in that club."

She paused a moment.

"What about working for the City Commissioner? Did he ever receive any political threats?"

"If he did, he didn't mention them to me. He was pretty behind-the-scenes."

JD pulled into the parking lot at City Hall. He found a space and killed the engine.

"Thank you for your time, Mrs. Gallagher. Again, I'm very sorry for your loss. If there's anything I can do, please don't hesitate to contact me."

"Just get the son-of-a-bitch who did this."

"I won't rest until we do."

We parked across the street and hustled toward the lobby. Flags rattled the flagpoles, and two towering palms guarded the entrance of the historic building. We climbed the steps and pushed inside.

Built in the 1930s, the building had recently been revamped. It was now the model of efficiency and environmental design with solar panels and reduced emissions. There were daily tours, and residents could explore the building and marvel at its advances. Home to the mayor and city commissioners, the renovation had cost upwards of $25 million.

Dario Johnson's office was in chaos after losing the Chief of Staff. An assistant behind a desk greeted us with a frazzled look. "How can I help you, gentlemen?"

I flashed my badge. "We'd like to speak with Mr. Johnson."

"One moment." She picked up the phone and dialed his extension. "Sir, there are two deputies here to see you." She listened for a second, then hung up the phone before responding. "He'll be with you shortly. Have a seat. Can I get you anything to drink? Bottled water?"

"No, thank you," I said. "A bit overwhelmed?"

A tense breath escaped her pretty lips. "That would be an understatement. I'm still trying to process what happened. It doesn't seem real. And now, I've suddenly been promoted to Chief of Staff. This is certainly not how I wanted to advance my career, but here we are."

"What's your name?"

"Mckenzie."

"I'm Tyson. This is JD."

She smiled, and we shook hands.

Mckenzie was early 20s with caramel eyes and light brown hair that dangled past her shoulders. She had full lips and adorable features. Not much makeup. A natural beauty.

"How well did you know Crosby?" I asked.

"We've all been working together since the election."

"Did you ever have any social interaction outside the office?"

"We'd all have a drink occasionally. But that was the extent of our friendship. I try to keep my professional life professional and my personal life personal. And no, I've never been to the Frisky Kitty, if that's what you're getting at?"

A moment later, Commissioner Johnson pulled open the door to his office. He gave a perfunctory smile. "Gentlemen, please, step inside."

He held the door as he ushered us into his office, offering us a seat. We shook hands and sat in front of the cherrywood desk with ornate carvings.

Dario sat in his chair, the American flag behind him on one side, the state flag on the other. Shafts of light filtered in through the blinds.

He folded his hands, and a grim frown tensed his face. "A terrible tragedy. Crosby was a fine young man and an excellent aid. He kept this office running and will be greatly missed."

Dario was in his late 50s with a terrible comb-over. It started in the back and spread forward, trying to approximate bangs. But it never really made it past the crown of his head. It looked like a monstrous hand made of gray hair grabbing his skull. He had a narrow face and a saggy chin. His brown eyes were puffy, and his teeth were overly whitened. Probably veneers.

"It is my solemn vow to put forth legislation that will ensure this kind of tragedy never happens again," he said, almost making a campaign speech. "These senseless crimes must stop, and I will not rest until Crosby's killer is brought to justice."

"Neither will we," I said.

"The full resources of my office are at your disposal."

"Thank you," I said. "We're wondering if this might be politically motivated."

The commissioner's face crinkled. "I can't imagine anyone attacking Crosby for grievances against my office. I'm polling very well in my district. I have the highest approval rating of any sitting commissioner." He didn't do a good job of hiding a proud smile.

His was one of several districts in Coconut Key.

Dario continued, "And I mean to shut down that establishment. Along with the other adult-oriented blights. That kind of debauchery is no good for Coconut Key. Brings in a bad element. Especially that Forgotten Fruit."

"Forbidden Fruit," I corrected.

"Whatever. It's the devil's playground. And it needs to be shut down."

*Forbidden Fruit* was one of JD's favorite places. I didn't mind it so much either.

---

## 8

We listened to the commissioner rant and rave, making empty promises to clean up the city and stop the violence. Unfortunately, he didn't have any useful insight into the case.

We thanked him for his time, said goodbye to Mckenzie, and headed across the island to speak with Heather Ingle. She lived in the *Sunbeam Shores* on Atlantic Avenue. Nice condos with a private beach—four stories, spacious balconies overlooking the ocean, a central heated pool and jacuzzi with towering palm trees, community gas grills, gym access, and clay tennis courts.

A little oasis.

We pulled into the lot and hopped out. "You know who she is, don't you?" JD said as we walked toward the main entrance.

I shrugged.

"She's John Ingle's daughter. Big hedge fund guy."

"That would explain the nice condo," I said.

At the call box, I dialed random numbers until someone answered. "Pizza delivery."

"I didn't order pizza."

"Is this 312?"

"No. It's 222."

"Can you buzz me in? They're not answering, and I've got deliveries to make."

A moment later, the magnetic lock released.

JD smiled and pulled open the lobby door. We stepped inside, found the elevators, and made our way up to the fourth floor. We stepped into the hallway and found Suite #412. I banged on the door, and a moment later, a soft voice asked, "Who is it?"

"Coconut County," I said, holding my badge to the peephole. "We'd like to talk to you about Crosby Gallagher."

The deadbolt unlatched, and Heather pulled open the door. She was a stunning blonde with pale skin and a tempting figure. Her golden hair spun in waves down to her shoulders. Her intense blue eyes looked us up and down. A skeptical look twisted her face. "You guys are cops?"

"We are a special crimes unit," JD said with a smile.

"Why do you want to talk to me?"

"You were dating Crosby, correct?" I said.

"Not really. We were... separated."

"When was the last time you spoke with him?"

"A couple days ago."

"That doesn't really sound separated."

Her eyes narrowed at me. "We had a complicated relationship."

"That's what I hear."

"Who did you hear that from?"

"Crosby's mother."

Her face tensed. "Well, I would take anything she says with a grain of salt."

"I take it you two didn't get along?"

Her face reddened. "She poisoned Crosby against me. Manipulative bitch."

"Tell us how you really feel," JD muttered.

"I feel like she stuck her nose where it didn't belong."

"Is that why things didn't work out?" I asked.

"It didn't work out because Crosby liked to stick his dick in everything that walked."

"Yet, you kept coming back to him."

"Matters of the heart are often difficult to control."

"So, it's hard for you to control your emotions?"

She glared at me, rage building. "That's not what I said."

"Have you ever been to the Frisky Kitty?"

"A few times. It really wasn't my thing. Crosby wanted an open relationship. I didn't."

"Understandable."

"If you ask me, he was trading down with some of the skanks in there. I mean, please, what was he doing with that old hag."

"Old hag?"

"That trampy cougar. Dawn."

"She was 36."

"Like I said. Old."

"How old are you?"

"23."

"Seems like you are pretty upset about his philandering."

Her eyes flicked between the two of us. "No. I wasn't upset at all." Her voice dripped with sarcasm. "Whatever gave you that idea?"

Heather was a petite, 5'3" heartbreaker. Not easily confused with a 6' gunman. But she did have the means to hire the job.

"How do you feel now that Crosby's gone?"

"What are you? My therapist?"

"Where were you last night?"

"I was with a girlfriend."

"Who?"

"None of your business."

"If you tell me who, I can corroborate your story."

Her face crinkled. "My story?"

"Jealous ex-lover storms into a swingers' bar and guns down the man that jilted her," JD postulated.

She laughed. "You can't possibly think that I was the shooter. I've never even held a gun before."

"No, but maybe you paid somebody to do it," I said.

Her brow knitted. "I didn't pay anybody to do anything. I have better things to spend my money on." She groaned with frustration. "If you must know, I was with Celeste last night. We went to Tide Pool, Turtles, and Bumper."

"Are you dating anybody else right now?"

"I don't see how my personal life is any of your business."

"We're trying to eliminate you as a suspect."

She huffed. "I have plenty of suitors."

"I'm sure. But of all your many *suitors*, who's the most obsessed?"

## 9

"Patrick Henry," Heather said after a moment's thought. "He's definitely in love with me. I only went out with him to make Crosby jealous."

"Maybe Patrick was jealous of Crosby," I said.

She pondered the thought. "You think maybe he did this?"

"Is that something he's capable of?"

She shrugged. "Who knows what someone else is capable of?"

"Did Patrick express any anger or make threats?"

"We'd only gone out a few times. But he was ready to lock it down." She cringed. "He was a little needy. Okay, a *lot* needy. He'd get upset if I didn't respond to him right away when he texted. Then he'd go off on me, accusing me of cheating on him. I said, 'Hang on, Buddy. We're not even together.'"

"I'll need contact information for him and your friend Celeste."

She pulled out her phone and texted me the information.

"You don't seem too broken up about Crosby's death," I said.

Her eyes narrowed at me. "We all grieve in different ways, Deputy. Life goes on. What do you want me to do, fall into a depression and never get out of bed again?" Her eyes misted, and she wiped the tears away just as they spilled over. "Crosby was very important to me. But he made the choice to disrespect the relationship. I refuse to get hung up on somebody who wouldn't commit to me."

"Fair enough." I told her to get in touch if she could think of anything else that might be helpful.

We left and headed back toward the elevator. I called Isabella, my handler at *Cobra Company*. It was the premier clandestine agency. With a network of global operatives and vast intelligence resources, they were perhaps more powerful than the three-letter agencies—and they were completely off the books.

"I need another favor," I said. "Can you get background information on Heather Ingle—cell phone records, bank transactions? You know the drill. Look for anything suspicious."

"Is this related to the mass shooting?"

"It is."

"I'll see what I can find out."

"Everything good in your world?"

She laughed. "You know better than to ask that. If things were good in my world, I'd be out of a job."

The spy world was a never-ending sea of chaos, one step away from disaster at any moment.

While I had her on the phone, I asked her to look up Patrick Henry's information.

"31. Works in IT. Lives on a 42-foot sportfish at Sandpiper Point. *Code is Cash*. You like him for a suspect?"

"Don't know yet."

Her fingers tapped a keyboard. "No criminal record. Couple speeding tickets. Looks clean."

"Can you track his phone?"

Her fingers danced across the keys again. A moment later, she responded, "Off the grid."

"What about Friday night at the time of the shooting?"

The keys rattled again. "Off the grid as well."

"I'm starting to like him more and more as a suspect."

"I'll dig around, see what I can find."

Isabella could usually find quite a lot.

I didn't want to ask too many favors. She'd been more than gracious to assist me in my cases, and I figured I was tipping the scales of our relationship. I had used up most of my good credit with her, and I was sure she'd call me one day to collect. But while I was asking, I thought I might as well go for another. "What do you know about Jean-Claude Juneau?"

Her fingers clacked the keys once more. "French Playboy. Family money. Started a few failed businesses, which ended up being tax write-offs. Owns one of the three Jewels of Aphrodite. Fascinating legend."

"I'm aware."

"Why are you asking?"

"He offered me a job."

"Don't you have your hands full without moonlighting?"

I gave her the details of the situation. "It will come under my jurisdiction anyway."

"Could be exciting."

"I don't need any more excitement."

She scoffed. "You crave it, or you wouldn't be in this line of work. Speaking of, I could use you back in the field full time."

"I like my life how it is."

She sighed exaggeratedly. "Fine."

"If you hear any chatter about someone moving on the jewel, give me a heads up."

"You got it."

I thanked her for the information and ended the call. We left the building, hopped into the Porsche, and headed to *Sandpiper Point*. It was home to tech types, investment gurus, crypto millionaires, and trust fund babies. Superyachts floated in slips, and there was always an elite party some-where. Patrick's 42-foot boat was small by comparison.

A massive party was in full effect aboard a 140-foot Italian superyacht. Girls in skimpy bikinis pranced around the foredeck with champagne flutes dangling from perfectly manicured hands. Teeny fabric disappeared into small crevices. Topless beauties lounged on sun pads, skin glistening with oil. Music pumped through speakers, and young guys did their best to win hearts.

Not a bad way to spend a Saturday afternoon.

We found *Code is Cash* and stepped into the cockpit. I banged on the salon door, but there was no response.

I banged again, and still no reply.

We scanned the marina, and JD suggested we investigate the party.

W e crossed the passerelle and stepped onto the aft deck of the *Aquanaught*. With people coming and going, nobody paid us any attention. We wandered through the crowd of pretty people. I didn't see anyone who resembled the DMV photo of the suspect.

I asked a passing girl in a teal bikini if she had seen Patrick Henry.

She shrugged. "I don't know half the people here."

"Neither do I," I said.

The brunette smiled. "Well, you know me, and that's all that matters."

She made a compelling case.

"I'm Tyson," I said with a smile.

"I'm Kendall. And you don't have a drink in your hand."

She took my hand and pulled me to the bar in the salon. Her hands were soft and warm. She shouted to the bartender over the music. "My friend is dry. He needs something wet."

The velvety words slipped from her tongue with delightfully naughty undertones. I could listen to her say the word *wet* all day long.

"Whiskey. Rocks," I said, not to be a party pooper. When in Rome, right?

JD was not about to let the opportunity slide. He ordered a whiskey, and I introduced him to my new friend.

Kendall's pretty blue eyes narrowed, surveying JD. "Where do I know you from?" Then it dawned on her. "You're in that band! I've seen your videos on the Internet."

Jack grinned. "Wild Fury."

"That's the one."

"And this here is my manager," he said, putting a hand on my shoulder.

"Celebrities. I'm impressed."

"I don't know if I'd call us celebrities," JD said, feigning modesty.

"Well, you're more famous than me."

"I bet you have legions of adoring fans."

Kendall smiled. With a hair flip, she said, "Well, that's true. I'm pretty popular on Instabook, just saying." She lifted her glass to toast. "To new friends."

The bartender poured the drinks and slid them across the counter.

We clinked glasses and sipped fine whiskey.

"So, how do you know Tristan?"

JD and I exchanged an awkward glance.

"We don't," I said, not wanting to get caught in a lie.

Her face crinkled with confusion. "So, you two just go around randomly crashing yacht parties?"

I smiled. "Pretty much."

"Cool. Is Patrick Henry real? Or was that a line?"

"It wasn't a line," I said with a chuckle.

"Well, let's see if we can find your friend. I'll give you a tour of the boat in the process."

We mingled through the salon, making our way forward, past a lounge area with a flatscreen TV.

"And how do you know Tristan?" I asked.

"He's my boyfriend."

I lifted a curious brow.

She chuckled. "I'm kidding." She paused. "If you promise not to tell anyone, I'll let you in on a little secret."

"I love secrets."

She whispered. "I don't know Tristan either."

"So, you're a party crasher too?"

A guilty shrug tugged her elegant shoulders. "I'm in town on business. Thought I'd see what kind of trouble I could get into."

"You look like you could get into a lot."

She lifted a sultry eyebrow. "What are you trying to say?"

I smiled. "It's okay. I seem to have an affinity for trouble."

We stepped onto the side deck, made our way forward, climbed the stairs, and arrived at the party on the foredeck. It was a feast for the eyes. Taught fabric stretched tight against toned bodies. Smooth skin shimmering. Buoyant assets jiggling.

I spotted Patrick Henry leaning against the gunwale, trying his best to impress a young lady.

"I think we found my friend," I said.

Kendall smiled. "It seems you have a decision to make."

"And what decision is that?"

"To hang out with your friend or to hang out with me."

"I like to have my cake and eat it too. How about I talk to my friend for a minute, then I come back, and you can show me the rest of the boat?"

She lifted a sassy eyebrow and pondered my suggestion for a moment. "How do you know I won't find a better option in the meantime?"

"I'm confident you will pick the best option."

"Are you saying you're my best option?"

I shrugged innocently.

"He's definitely your best option," JD said, backing me up like every good wingman should.

"I could always introduce you to my friend," I said.

She glanced across the foredeck at Patrick, then her sultry eyes flicked back to me. "Is he really your friend?"

I leaned in and whispered, "He's a suspect in a multiple homicide."

She giggled, not realizing I was serious. "Well, then, I definitely *have* to meet him."

We meandered across the deck, past the bevy of nude sunbathers. I pulled my badge from my pocket and stuck it in Patrick's face. "Coconut County. Need to ask you a few questions."

The girl he was talking to took the opportunity to leave. I don't think she was that interested, anyway.

Patrick's face tensed. "Why do you want to talk to me?"

Kendall leaned to JD and whispered, "Is that a real badge?"

"Yep, and we're real cops."

She thought about it for a moment, then made an impressed face. "Cool."

"Where were you last night?" I asked.

Patrick shifted uncomfortably.

## 11

"Who cares?" Patrick asked with a scowl.

"Have you been living under a rock?" I asked. "You realize there was a mass shooting last night, right?"

"So? What's that got to do with me?"

"Tell me where you were, provide a solid alibi, and maybe we can rule you out as a suspect?"

"A suspect?" He lifted an incredulous brow.

"Heather Ingle's ex-boyfriend was among the victims."

His face crinkled. "So?"

"You dated Heather Ingle."

"So?"

I shrugged. "Maybe you wanted him out of the picture."

"Let me get this straight. You think I was jealous of Crosby, so I walked into a swingers' bar and filled him, and everyone around him, full of lead?"

"So, you do watch the news?"

"I didn't walk into that place and go postal."

"Where were you?"

"I don't have to answer you. I don't have to say anything to you."

"No, you don't. But it might be a little easier."

"Easier for who? You?"

"I get suspicious when people get this combative. I'm starting to think maybe we're on the right track." I glanced at JD.

He nodded in agreement.

Patrick's annoyed eyes flicked between the two of us. "I was at home on my yacht."

"Alone?"

"Not all night. I had a lady friend come over at midnight."

"Want to give me her name?"

"No."

If I was a gambling man, and I am, I'd wager there was no lady friend. "Why was your phone off the grid?"

"You tracked my phone?"

I said nothing and kept staring at him.

"Don't you need a warrant for something like that?"

I ignored him. "I just find it odd that your phone was off the grid at the time of the murders.

"It's not illegal to turn your phone off, is it? I turn my phone off all the time when I'm not using it. It's off right now."

"Why do you turn it off?"

"It saves battery. Besides, you know how much electromagnetic radiation one of these things emits? I'm keeping that in my pocket all day long next to my balls. What's that doing to my balls? I don't know about you, but I like my balls. I'm not microwaving them just so I can receive up-to-the-minute texts."

"It's non-ionizing radiation."

"Yeah, that's what they say. But what's really going on? How do we really know what all this technology is doing to us? All these Wi-Fi signals and cell towers are cooking our brains."

"So, you were home aboard your *yacht*," I said in air quotes. "And you have no alibi."

"I don't need an alibi. I didn't do anything." He glared at us, his face red. "I'm done talking to you. Got any other questions? Talk to my lawyer."

He pushed off the gunwale and marched away, storming aft.

I exchanged a glance with JD, and he shrugged.

"Do you guys really think he's the active shooter?" Kendall asked.

"Hard to say. People have done crazier things to eliminate a romantic rival."

"That's kind of freaky. What if he comes back here an shoots up the place?" She smirked. "Maybe you should stick around to protect me."

I smiled. "I could be persuaded. How about that tour of the boat?"

I was more than happy to follow little Miss Perky through the boat as she gave me a tour of the luxurious appointments. The sleek windswept lines, the large windows, the plush furniture. I was looking forward to checking out a cozy guest cabin with her.

She rattled off facts and figures about the boat's construction and design elements.

"You're making this stuff up, aren't you?"

She smirked. "Well, I've never been on this boat before, so cut me some slack."

I chuckled.

She led us down a companionway. "And here we have a VIP stateroom." She opened the hatch and peered inside.

"I'm going to get a drink," JD said, taking his cue to leave.

"As you can see, it has a queen berth, an en suite, hanging storage lockers, and a fold-down TV," Kendall said.

"But is the bed comfortable?"

"Maybe we should find out."

We sneaked inside, and Kendall locked the hatch. It didn't look like anyone was currently living in the VIP stateroom. The dresser drawers were empty. We pretended to look around for a moment.

Music thumped through the bulkheads.

We stared at each other.

She stalked toward me, mischief in her eyes. I liked mischief. I liked it a lot.

"Would you like to continue the tour? Or would you like to stay here for a minute?"

"This might take more than a minute."

A naughty smirk curled her face. "Good."

She lifted on her tiptoes and planted her juicy lips against mine. They were pillowy soft. I put a hand on the small of her back and pressed her body against mine. Warm desire radiated between us. Our slick tongues danced, and my hands found joyous mounds of flesh. The room pulsed with the possibilities of lustful adventure.

The captain woke from his slumber, ready for action. Conditions were looking favorable for an amphibious landing when Daniels called.

I broke from our sensual embrace and answered the phone.

"Where are you two nitwits?"

"Running down a lead," I said.

"We've got another situation."

# 12

"You don't really have to go?" Kendall pouted. "The party is just getting started."

She looked at me with those adorable blue eyes, her full lips beckoning.

"Sorry, duty calls. Can we connect another time?"

She shrugged playfully. "I don't know, Deputy. Look around. Lots of options."

"I don't see any other options in here."

"There's a whole world outside."

I grinned. "You look like you've got a good eye. I'm sure you know quality when you see it."

She smiled. "I do."

I gave her my card. She studied it carefully.

"You should use that."

"Maybe I will. Maybe I won't," she said coyly.

I smirked and left the compartment. I found JD in the salon talking to a few cuties. A quizzical look twisted his face. "Well, this seems a bit... premature."

I scowled at him. "Daniels called."

He frowned. "So much for a little Saturday afternoon fun."

He excused himself from the ladies, and we headed aft. I glanced over my shoulder at Kendall as she entered the salon. She wiggled her fingers, and I tried not to think about what I was missing.

We crossed the passerelle to the dock and hustled to the parking lot.

Jack said, "This job gets in the way sometimes, doesn't it?"

"We wouldn't have been on that boat otherwise."

"True. Fate is a strange mistress."

We cruised across the island to the posh neighborhood of *Stingray Bay* and twisted through the well-maintained streets, past luxury mansions and towering palm trees. Driveways were filled with shiny new cars and SUVs. Lawn crews maintained yards within millimeters of perfection.

It wasn't hard to find the trouble spot. Red and blues flickered, and an ambulance was on the scene. Neighbors gathered in the street, gawking at the spectacle.

JD pulled to the curb a house down, and we hopped out and hustled to the McMansion. A white Mercedes SUV sat in the circular drive, and a black BMW sedan was parked by the garage.

Mendoza was at the front door. "They're in the bedroom."

We stepped into the cavernous foyer lined with Italian marble. A spiral staircase twisted to the second floor. Camera flashes spilled down a hallway that emptied into the living room. Abstract art hung from the walls in the spacious area. It had an open floor plan and seamlessly blended with the kitchen.

We made our way through the sprawling estate, following the flashes to the master bedroom.

A woman in her mid 30s with strawberry-blonde hair lay atop a four-post bed, her lifeless eyes staring at the ceiling.

Brenda examined the remains, and Dietrich snapped photos. A couple of EMTs loitered.

A distraught man approaching 40 stood nearby, watching in horror from the corner of the room. He was thin with dark hair and eyes. I figured him for the husband.

My phone buzzed with an encrypted text from Jean-Claude. *[We are set to transport Sunday. Details will follow shortly. Stay on alert status. I'll give you the exact time as we draw near. Are we confirmed?]*

Jean-Claude was smart to keep details unknown until the last minute.

[Confirmed] I replied, then focused my attention on the scene at hand. "What happened?"

"I don't know," the husband said. "I came home and found Miranda like this. She wasn't breathing. I called 911. The EMTs attempted to resuscitate her."

"She was non-responsive when we got to her," an EMT said. "She had no pulse or respiration. Her airways were clear. We used a defibrillator, but she was gone."

"No visible signs of trauma," Brenda said.

"How long has she been deceased?" I asked.

"At least two hours."

"We got here 30 minutes ago," the EMT said.

I looked at the husband. "And your name is?"

"Garrett. Garrett Clark." He looked dazed.

"What time did you discover her?" I asked.

"I guess it was 45 minutes ago. You can check the phone records for an exact time."

I didn't notice any drugs or prescription pill bottles on the nightstand. I snapped on a pair of nitrile gloves, then pulled open the drawer by the bed. It contained a compact 9mm, a tube of sex lube, and a bible. Quite the interesting combination.

Garrett's eyes rounded. "What are you doing?"

"I'm surveying the scene."

"I haven't given you permission to search my house."

I ignored his protest. "Was your wife taking any prescription medication?"

"Not that I'm aware of."

"No antidepressants, sleeping pills, insulin, heart medication?"

"No."

"Did she use any drugs or alcohol?"

"Miranda drank, but she never did any illegal drugs." Garrett paused. "I mean, she smoked a little herb every now and then."

I stepped into the master bathroom and fumbled through drawers and cabinets, further irritating Garrett. He followed and hovered in the doorway.

The bathroom was tastefully done with travertine tile. There was a walk-in shower stall, and a Jacuzzi tub with a flatscreen TV mounted on the wall. It was the perfect place to lounge in a bubble bath and watch your favorite show.

"I don't understand what you're looking for," Garrett said.

"I'm looking for anything that might have led to your wife's current condition."

"I'm telling you, she didn't use prescription or illegal drugs."

"Perhaps we should step into the living room and give the investigators space to work."

His face tensed, but he complied.

JD and I followed him out of the bedroom and down the hallway into the spacious living room. Large windows offered a view of the pool and the canal beyond, which was home to a 70-foot sportfish.

"Where were you before you came home?" I asked.

"I ran to the store to pick up items for this afternoon. I was planning on grilling hamburgers."

"And you called 911 right away?"

"Once I discovered Miranda, yes."

I lifted a curious brow. "Once you discovered her?"

"I came inside, put the groceries away, then I sat on the couch and watched TV. I didn't hear Miranda. Her car was here, but it seemed awfully quiet. I went to the bedroom to see if she was here, and that's when I found her."

"How long were you home before you found her?"

"Maybe 30 minutes."

"I see." I was somewhat skeptical of his story.

His eyes narrowed at me. "What do you *see*?"

"How was your relationship with your wife?"

His face crinkled. "Why do you ask?"

"Usually when a spouse turns up dead under mysterious circumstances, I get curious."

"Mysterious circumstances?"

"Your wife seems to have been an otherwise healthy mid-30s woman in the prime of her life. Now she's not breathing. That's mysterious."

"Look, I don't know what you're getting at. I told you, I came home and called 911 as soon as I discovered her body."

"I noticed your wife wasn't wearing a wedding ring."

That hung in the air for a moment.

Garrett tensed. He took a breath, then exhaled. "Okay, things haven't been the greatest around here. Miranda filed for divorce a few weeks ago."

Alarm bells went off.

"Your wife filed for divorce, then turns up dead a few weeks later. I'd definitely call that mysterious." I looked at JD. "Would you call that mysterious?"

He nodded.

"On second thought, maybe it's not so mysterious after all," I said, my eyes staring into Garrett's.

"What are you getting at?"

"I'm just saying, it's rather convenient for you, isn't it?"

His cheeks flushed, and his jaw tightened. "There is nothing convenient about the fact that my wife is dead."

His eyes brimmed, and I couldn't tell if it was from sadness or anger.

"You've got to admit, it looks a little funny." I was trying to push his buttons.

It was working.

"There is nothing funny about this, Deputy."

My eyes surveyed the area. The open floor plan gave a clear view to the kitchen and the center island, topped with marble. I caught sight of a red box of Valentine's Day chocolates on the countertop.

I moved across the living room and examined the box of square chocolates. They were filled with creamy, syrupy

goodness. Multiple flavors—dark chocolate and milk chocolate, filled with cherry, strawberry, cream, you name it. Half
of the candies had been eaten, and empty wrappers
remained.

"Were you eating the chocolates or just your wife?"

"I don't eat sugar."

"Where did the chocolates come from?"

"I bought them for Miranda yesterday."

"You bought your wife a box of Valentine's chocolates when
she's divorcing you?"

"I love my wife, Deputy. The divorce wasn't my idea. I was
desperate to get her back."

I leaned over and sniffed the chocolate, trying to detect any
unusual odors. I waved over one of the forensics guys and
told him to bag the chocolate as evidence.

"You think the chocolate was poisoned?" Garrett asked.

"I think it's a distinct possibility."

Panic tensed his face. "I didn't poison them. The box was
still shrink-wrapped when I gave it to Miranda."

"It's too bad she's not around to verify your story."

He glared at me. "I didn't poison my wife!"

If he was telling the truth, we had a serious problem on our
hands.

## 13

In an abundance of caution, I contacted the grocery store where Garrett bought the Valentine's chocolates and had them pull the stock until the lab results came back.

I called Teagan as well and told her to throw the chocolates out just in case.

"Oh, so you're trying to poison me?" Teagan teased.

"Yes, it's all part of my plan to get rid of my best employee."

"I could just quit, you know. Then you wouldn't be my boss anymore," she said in a flirty tone.

"Hmm. Think of the possibilities," I said, amused.

"Do you really think these could be contaminated?"

"Erring on the side of caution. I'll let you know when we get lab results."

I hung up and dialed Denise.

"Good. I didn't need the sugar anyway," she said when I informed her. "And you're a dick, by the way."

"What did I do?"

"You made me cry."

"I thought you weren't going to open it at work."

"Yeah, well, curiosity got the best of me." She paused. "Thank you. It was sweet. You're important to me too."

"Now I'm getting misty."

"Shut up." She paused. "And you know I'm going to call Teagan to compare notes. If you wrote us both the same thing, you're in trouble."

I laughed. "Go ahead, call her."

"I just might."

I ended the call, and Garrett accompanied us to the station. We put him into an interrogation room. This time, his responses were on video. He was mostly cooperative, though highly upset and annoyed. We kept him in that tiny room for a long time, trying to elicit a confession.

He was more than ready to leave.

15 minutes in that room was enough to drive most people batshit. Everything about it was designed to unnerve. The harsh fluorescent lighting, the freezing temperature, the sound dampening, the odd angles—the walls and trim weren't quite straight. It wasn't funhouse askew, but just enough to make you question your sanity.

"How many times are you guys going to ask me the same questions? My answers aren't going to change. Is this how you treat every spouse when the love of their life dies?"

"I know this is a difficult time," I said. "I apologize if you find these questions accusatory. We're just trying to be thorough."

"I've been here for three hours. I've answered every question. I've done everything you've asked me to do. I want to go home and grieve in peace, if you don't mind."

"You're not under arrest. You're free to leave at any time."

He gave me an exasperated look. "I've given you enough of my time."

He stood up and pushed away from the table.

I moved to the door, knocked on it, and a guard buzzed us out. I held the door for Garrett, and he shot me an annoyed glance as he stepped into the hallway.

JD and I followed and watched him walk away. He turned the corner and disappeared.

"What do you think?" JD muttered.

"I'm reserving judgment until the toxicology report comes back."

"Speaking of poison," JD said, looking at his watch. "It's just about happy hour. You hear from that new lady friend of yours?"

"Not yet."

"The night is young," he said with optimism.

We filled out reports, then headed to *Wetsuit* for the special. JD ordered the local yellowtail snapper with lemon butter and capers, and I went with the seafood linguini with clams, shrimp, baby scallops, and spinach with a sherry cream sauce. We sipped fine whiskey and took in the scenery. The amaretto coconut cream pie was hard to turn down.

With full bellies, we headed to the practice studio to meet up with the band. *Wild Fury* was headlining at *Sonic Temple* tonight.

We pulled into the lot in the warehouse district. The usual band of miscreants loitered out front, smoking cigarettes and drinking beer.

The sound of practicing bands spilled into the lot as we made our way toward the entrance. The miscreants high-fived JD, and we pushed into the dim hallway that reeked of beer and Mary Jane.

Inside the practice space, the band prepped their gear for the gig. Dizzy was happy to have his stolen guitar back. We recovered it from Jesse Jams, who said she purchased the axe from Johnny Wicked, the guitarist of *Lithium Panic*. They were a pop-punk band currently on tour. I had been unable to reach them, so we were at a standstill in our pursuit of the gear thieves.

*Lithium Panic* would return to Coconut Key eventually. I wasn't sure if they were responsible for the string of thefts or if Johnny Wicked had purchased the guitar unknowingly. I did notice that since they were out of town, there hadn't been any more robberies. Maybe that was their whole MO —steal gear to fund their tour and rock 'n' roll lifestyle.

There were better ways to make money.

We loaded the gear into the band van and headed over to *Sonic Temple* to set up for soundcheck. The band ran through a couple songs, and the sound guy set the level. It was old hat. *Wild Fury* was a regular at the venue, so it didn't take much to dial in the sound.

Afterward, we left *Sonic Temple* and decided to pregame at *O'Grady's*. The Irish pub was a block off of Oyster Avenue and wasn't as touristy. There were dartboards and pool tables and cozy booths. The music was always good, and Effie behind the bar had a heavy pour. The drinks were cheap, and the vibe was good.

JD bought a round for the guys, and we all lifted our glasses to toast. "To Wild Fury."

"Wild Fury!" We responded in unison.

We clinked glasses and indulged in the fine amber liquid.

We were halfway through the second round when Denise buzzed my phone. "Hey, I found something interesting. I've been doing some digging into the Frisky Kitty victims. It seems Tara Ward was a prosecution witness in the upcoming murder trial of Benito Diaz."

I lifted a curious brow. "Tell me more."

"I think she could have been the target."

"I'd say that's definitely cause for further investigation. Nice work."

"Thank you," she said with a smile in her voice. "I just talked to her husband, Ed. Poor guy. He didn't even know she was swinging."

"Is it really swinging if he doesn't know? Sounds more like cheating to me."

"He said Tara was supposed to be in acting class that night."

"Tell me about the murder Tara witnessed."

"Gang-related. Benito Diaz of the Disciples of Hell beat and stabbed Marco Medina. He was a member of Satan's Children."

"Sounds like two outstanding organizations," I snarked. "Where did this take place?"

"On Ocean Avenue near Taffy Beach."

"And Tara Ward was the sole witness?"

"I think so."

"Was there any surveillance footage?"

"I'll see what I can dig up."

I asked, "Who's prosecuting the case?"

"Marla Mackey."

"Any particular motive for the murder?"

"Who knows? It doesn't take much for tensions to flare. Look at somebody the wrong way, and they want to kill you."

I gave a grim grunt. "What can you tell me about the Disciples of Hell?"

"Smalltime street gang. The usual—drugs, prostitution, extortion. Pepe Vasquez leads the organization."

"Dig up everything you can on them. We'll talk to Tara's husband, Ed Ward, tomorrow. Did I tell you how great you are?"

"I never get tired of hearing it."

I chuckled and ended the call.

We finished our drinks, and JD paid the tab.

"I'm still waiting on my autographed T-shirt," Effie said to JD.

"I will bring it the next time I come," JD promised. "You want me to put you on the guest list for tonight?"

"If you can find somebody to work the bar for me," she joked.

We left and headed back to *Sonic Temple*. We caught the end of the *Manic Deadbeats*, then hung out in the green room while the staff changed the stage.

*Wild Fury* was met with roaring applause when they finally took the stage. The house was packed as usual, and the band thundered out their unique brand of party rock anthems.

Afterward, we returned to the *Avventura* for the usual after-show soirée, but something in the parking lot caught my eye.

JD had a mischievous grin on his face.

*Diver Down* was closed, but Teagan was still inside wrapping up. There weren't many cars in the lot.

Jack parked the Porsche next to a 1970 Plymouth 'Cuda. We hopped out and marveled at the muscle car from a bygone era.

Painted in Plum Crazy Purple with white vinyl interior, the vehicle looked brand-spanking new. It had a matte black hood and a rear spoiler. The stance was mean and aggressive.

The custom license plate read D3VST8R.

"You like that?" JD asked.

"I love it," I said, marveling at the beast.

"I figure there might be instances where we need something besides the Porsche to get around in."

I gave him a curious look. "You bought this? This is your surprise?"

He smiled. "I present to you, the *Devastator*. It's got a 6.2 Gen III V8 Hellcat Hemi crate engine rated at 707 hp, paired with a six-speed manual transmission. Makes 650 foot-pounds of torque. It has a custom exhaust and long tube headers."

The resto-mod had been completely redone. The interior got a facelift with all new gauges and dials. It was a new car with an old body.

"You should have seen this before," JD said. "It was a hunk of junk. Had my buddy do the restoration. New chassis, rack and pinion steering, coil overs, Brembo brakes with slotted rotors, forged aluminum rims. And that's not even the best part."

"What's the best part?"

"Bulletproof doors and windows. Run-flat tires. This thing is a tank."

After some of JD's previous close calls, I didn't blame him a bit for wanting an armored vehicle.

"The 707 hp should offset the added weight."

The guys in the band showed up along with a plethora of groupies. They all swarmed around the car, taking in its magnificence.

They certainly didn't make them like this anymore.

Teagan joined us in the parking lot and handed the keys to JD. "Bobby dropped it off earlier. I want you to be aware of how much self-discipline it took for me not to take a spin around the block in this car."

"You can drive it any time," JD said.

Her eyes rounded, and excitement glowed her face. "Really?"

"Absolutely."

"Don't say that. I'll drive it every day. You know me and muscle cars."

JD grinned.

"Why don't you take Tyson for a spin?"

He tossed the keys back to her. She had a smile so bright it could outshine the sun.

She marched around to the driver's door, pulled it open, and slid behind the wheel. She looked like she was about to climax the moment her pert cheeks touched the seat.

I slid into the seat beside her and pulled the door shut with a thunk.

Teagan cranked the engine up, and it growled with ferocity. We both exchanged a grin. The exhaust burbled, and the pistons pinged. The car rumbled. Even at idle, you could feel the potential power.

Teagan backed out of the space, and the crowd parted.

"Can I do a burnout?"

"This car was built for burnouts," JD said, standing beside the car.

Teagan smiled and rolled out of the lot. She turned on the road and stood still, revving the engine.

No cars were on the road at this hour.

A grin tugged her plump lips. She dropped the clutch and hammered the gas. Tires spun, and clouds of white smoke billowed from the wheel wells. The smell of rubber and exhaust filled the air, and the engine roared.

She painted a streak of black against the asphalt, then let off the gas and giggled as the cloud of smoke dissipated.

I'm sure the noise woke up everyone in the marina.

We cruised into the night, the windows down, the wind swirling around. We didn't need the stereo—the sound of the engine was music.

"I could definitely get used to this," Teagan said.

"Looks good on you."

Everything looked good on Teagan.

We drove around the island, then brought the car back to the marina. By this time, the revelers had moved to the *Avventura*.

Teagan pulled into a parking space and killed the engine. She soaked in its glory for one last moment. She dreamed, "One of these days…"

We hopped out of the car, and she dangled the keys from her pretty fingers. "I hate to give these back."

She dropped them into my palm, then lifted on her tiptoes and kissed me on the cheek. "Thanks for the ride."

"Thank JD."

She spun around and sauntered to her car.

"Want to come back to the boat for a drink?"

"Some other time. I'm beat."

I couldn't blame her. She worked nonstop. It was probably a good thing anyway. She looked too delicious.

I watched her get into her car and drive away, then headed to the boat to join the party. It lasted until the wee hours of the morning.

I settled in early and tried to get some sleep, despite the thumping music seeping through the bulkheads. We were scheduled to escort the Jewel of Aphrodite from the FBO at the Coconut Key airport to the museum. In theory, it should have been straightforward. But nothing is ever as easy as it seems.

## 14

Jean-Claude called early in the morning on the encrypted messaging app. I grabbed the phone from the nightstand and tried to sound awake when I asked, "Is everything still moving according to plan?"

"I will arrive in Coconut Key within the hour. We will move forward with the plan as discussed."

Jean-Claude and I had gone over the finer points of the operation through a series of text messages. I was relatively confident in the plan.

"I'll see you there," I said.

I ended the call and sprung out of bed. I showered, got dressed, then banged on the hatch to JD's stateroom. "We're *Oscar Mike* in 15."

It was slang for *on the move.*

He groaned.

I hustled into the galley and threw a breakfast burrito into the microwave. No time to fix breakfast for the gang. I put on a pot of coffee, and the invigorating scent wafted through the galley.

JD emerged a few minutes later, looking bleary-eyed, his long blonde hair ratted. "Your client likes to work on short notice."

"Only dish out information when absolutely necessary."

We stuffed breakfast burritos in our mouths, then prepped for the mission. We both wore bulletproof vests under our shirts. I press checked my weapon and stuffed a few extra magazines into cargo pockets. JD pulled his hair into a ponytail and covered it with a ball cap. I wore a pair of mirrored sunglasses. We looked like a cross between beach bums and feds.

Nobody else was stirring on the *Avventura* except Buddy and Fluffy. There were a few groupies passed out on settees, and the salon was littered with beer bottles. The supply of liquor behind the bar had been seriously depleted.

I took Buddy out for a quick walk, then escorted him back to the boat. JD and I hustled down the dock to the parking lot. We had decided to take the Devastator since it was armored. But there was no way a grown man could fit comfortably in the back seat. It seemed smaller than the Porsche.

I pulled on my helmet and gloves and straddled my sport-bike. I cranked up the engine and revved the throttle. The exhaust rattled a high-strung note.

I followed JD to the FBO at the Coconut Key airport. I hugged the tank, and the crotch rocket begged to be unleashed.

It was a calm, peaceful morning. Warm rays of sun beamed down. Wind swirled around as we cruised down the road.

Something told me the calm of the morning wouldn't last long.

We pulled into the FBO and found a place to park. JD and I casually walked into the terminal, took a seat in lounge chairs, and waited. We watched planes take off and land.

I spotted another gentleman entering the terminal, wearing shorts, a T-shirt, a ball cap, and sunglasses. A backpack hung from his shoulders. He pushed into the men's restroom.

Jean-Claude arrived on schedule 15 minutes later. His Slipstream G-750 rolled onto the tarmac by the terminal. A flight attendant opened the door and lowered the stairs. Several security guards in suits exited the plane, surveying the area. They wore dark sunglasses and had earpieces. They looked like secret servicemen.

That was our cue.

JD and I stood up, walked across the terminal, and pushed into the public restroom. I placed an *out of order* sign on the door as we entered.

The guy with the backpack had never left. He waited for us by the far stall. He'd changed from his T-shirt and shorts into a Navy blue DiFiori suit. He wore a Rolex Oyster Perpetual that he wasn't wearing when he entered. He was the spitting image of Jean-Claude.

"You Mark?" I asked.

He nodded.

We shook hands and made introductions.

I couldn't help but stare at the guy. The likeness was remarkable. Jean-Claude had coordinated the whole thing.

"Are you from Coconut Key?"

Mark shook his head. "No. I flew in yesterday."

"You work for Jean-Claude on a regular basis?"

"All the time."

"How many doubles does he have?"

"I'm not at liberty to say," he said with a slight grin.

A moment later, the real Jean-Claude entered the restroom with his two security guards. At least, I think it was the real Jean-Claude.

He shook my hand with a warm smile. "Deputy Wild, great to meet you in person."

"Likewise. This is my associate, Jack Donovan."

The two exchanged pleasantries.

An aluminum briefcase dangled from Jean-Claude's left hand. He handed the case to Mark, obviously a decoy. Jean-Claude dug into his pocket and handed me a jewelry box.

"This is it, I assume?"

Jean-Claude nodded.

I opened the box and surveyed the precious jewel. It had a mesmerizing quality. There was an energy about it. I wouldn't spend my fortune on it, but I could see the allure.

I closed the box and slipped it into my pocket.

Jean-Claude changed into a T-shirt and shorts identical to those Mark had worn. He put on sunglasses and a ball cap, completing the transformation.

Mark left with the bodyguards.

It was a cunning ruse.

The decoy left the terminal and hopped into an armored limousine that waited for them at the curb.

We stayed in the restroom a few minutes before exiting. JD took the lead, and I brought up the rear. We stepped into the terminal and surveyed the area for threats, then headed outside.

We casually walked across the lot to the Devastator.

Jean-Claude was impressed. "Nice ride."

JD explained the car's attributes with the smile of a proud owner.

I hopped onto my bike, pulled on my helmet and gloves, and cranked up the engine.

Jean-Claude took the front passenger seat of the Devastator, and JD climbed behind the wheel. He fired up the engine, pulled out of the space, and rolled out of the lot.

I kept my head on a swivel as I followed, but I didn't antici- pate much trouble. The only way someone would make us is if Jean-Claude had a leak in his organization. I hadn't told anyone except JD, and even he didn't know the full details until it played out.

We headed toward the museum, but it didn't take us long to come upon the chaos. The traffic ahead slowed, and the sound of gunfire clattered. Muzzle flash flickered.

It was game on.

## 15

B lack SUVs had boxed in the limousine and forced it to the shoulder. Masked gunmen surrounded the car, blasting it with submachine guns.

Metal popped and pinged as they peppered the vehicle.

Bullets cratered the resistant glass.

Gun smoke drifted on the breeze.

It was a full-scale assault.

I pulled off my helmet, called Daniels, and told him to send patrol units and to get Tango One in the air. I had to fight the urge to hop off the bike and advance down the row of red taillights to engage the thugs, but my priority was Jean-Claude and the jewel.

The onslaught continued.

Molten copper blasted the limo, chipping the paint, flaking the bulletproof glass.

The limousine driver angled for a gap between the SUVs. He mashed the pedal. The tires squealed, and body panels crinkled as the limousine rammed into the SUVs, trying to widen the gap between the front bumper of one and the rear bumper of another.

Smoke wafted from the wheel wells as the rear tires spun against the asphalt.

The thugs kept peppering the car with bullets, trying to take out the driver.

Terrified drivers in other cars crouched below dashes.

Eventually, the limo wedged open a gap between the vehicles and squeezed through. Paint peeled, and metal squealed. Sparks flew as the vehicle broke free.

The thugs continued firing as the limo raced away.

The sound of distant sirens rumbled, and I heard the thump of rotor blades approach.

The thugs hopped into their SUVs. Tires barked as they launched away. They didn't bother giving chase. Their allotted time was up. Escape was their only option now. The mission had failed.

Traffic began to move again once the scene cleared.

We drove past the battlefield. Bits of glass and plastic littered the ground. Tire tracks stained the asphalt.

From what I could tell, no one had gotten hurt.

All things considered, it was still a good day. Though my heart rate was slightly elevated. I had to admit, Jean-

Claude's plan seemed brilliant. Nobody gave us a second glance. And I hoped it would stay that way.

I followed the Devastator to the museum.

We did a drive-by to make a threat assessment. It looked clear when we passed, so we spun around and pulled into the lot. JD drove to the front entrance. Jean-Claude hopped out, and I pulled up behind them.

For security reasons, the museum was closed.

I scanned the area as Jean-Claude called his crew. "Is everyone okay?"

"We're good here," Damon said, his voice filtering through the speakerphone. "The driver is a little rattled. What do you want us to do?"

Jean-Claude looked at me for guidance.

"If the vehicle is drivable, tell them to head to the station. If not, I'll send deputies to their location."

He relayed the information to Damon, and they agreed to go to the Sheriff's Department. The forensic team could pull slugs from the vehicle and run ballistics. "Once you finish with the police, check in at the hotel and do a security sweep."

I called Daniels again. "Was Tango One able to spot the shooters?"

"Found the abandoned vehicles, but the shooters got away clean. You get a good look at those guys?"

"No."

He grumbled, then said, "I'll keep you posted."

I ended the call, and we marched up the steps. Jack left the car parked up front.

Museum security greeted us at the entrance and unlocked the door. Jean-Claude had kept the curator, Avery Blanchett, updated.

Avery was with four uniformed museum security guards— all of whom looked like they might have a little trouble passing a standard physical fitness test. The most action they typically saw was keeping kids from touching the Monets.

"So great to meet you face to face," Avery said as she shook hands with Jean-Claude.

"The pleasure is all mine," he replied with a charming smile.

I scanned the interior and kept an eye on the parking lot while the guards locked the entrance.

Avery was an intriguing brunette about 5'4". An elegant beauty with refined features and a lofty air about her. She spoke with that affectation that all art snobs seem to possess. Avery had forgotten more about art than most people would ever learn in a lifetime. She had beautiful brown eyes and outstanding *posture*.

"I trust you had an uneventful journey," Avery said.

"I can't say that for my entire staff, but we are here, unharmed."

She gave Jean-Claude a curious look.

"You'll hear all about it on the news, I'm sure."

"I hope everything is okay?" Her face crinkled with concern.

"An attempt was made. The jewel is safe, and so is my team. That's all that matters."

"Good. Let me show you to the gallery."

Avery led us through the museum to the second floor. Trailing behind her wasn't a bad view. We passed masterworks of art—pieces by Rembrandt, Cézanne, Matisse, van Gogh, and Picasso, to name a few.

It was a sprawling complex with various exhibits and significant paintings from renowned collections. There was a gift shop, cafe, auditorium, and a small theater. There were plazas and gardens with manicured hedgerows. It was a place of enlightenment and education.

Avery escorted us to a gallery with several priceless gemstones. In the center was an empty glass box atop a pedestal just waiting to display the prized Jewel of Aphrodite. The area had been blocked off with stanchions in anticipation of our arrival. The security staff did a sweep of the area, then JD and I entered and cleared the room as well.

I examined the protective glass case. "Tell me about your security protocols here?"

## 16

"We have a state-of-the-art security system," Avery said. She pointed to the cameras in the ceiling. "24-hour monitoring, infrared switchable. Predictive behavioral algorithms can detect and track suspicious activity. There are pressure-sensitive pads in the floor and laser motion detectors. This case is bullet-proof glass. It's secured by a 2,500-pound electromagnetic lock which is only accessible via this biometric pad." She pointed to the fingerprint scanner on the pedestal. There was a numeric keypad above it.

Avery placed her thumb on the pad. The lock clicked free. She lifted the glass case from the pedestal. The bottom of the glass was rimmed with metal.

She smiled with pride, then put the case back on the pedestal and locked it. "Mr. Juneau can program this keypad himself. No one else will have access. The walls are lined with carbon steel, and carbon steel doors will secure the room during the night and in case of emergency. Of course, we have the requisite fire suppression systems in place as well."

"That's not secure," I said, pointing to the display case.

Avery's face went long, and concern filled Jean-Claude's eyes.

Avery grew defensive and scoffed. "And who are you again?"

"Right now, he's my Chief of Security," Jean-Claude said.

"Go ahead," Avery said. "Try to remove the glass."

"The glass isn't the weakest point. The keypad is," I said, pointing.

Avery's brow knitted, and she shook her head. "That keypad is entirely secure. It has a tamper sensor, and the wireless connection is encrypted."

"Encryption can be hacked. Networks can be compromised."

"Not this network," she said with confidence.

"Every network is vulnerable. And I can get into that keypad within 30 seconds."

She scoffed again. "By all means. Show me."

"I don't have the proper tools."

She sneered at me. "Why don't you get the proper tools and give it a shot? I'd bet my job that you can't get into that case."

"You must not like your job."

"I love my job. And I intend on keeping it." She looked at Jean-Claude. "I can assure you, this keypad is the latest in security technology. It cannot be breached. In the unlikely event that it is, there is no way someone is going to make it from this gallery to the outside. At the push of a button, the room will seal, and my security staff will handle the situation. Test the system for yourself, Jean-Claude."

Avery punched her code into the keypad, then placed her thumb on the fingerprint scanner. The lock released with a click, and she pressed the memory button twice. "You can now set your own personal code. We will leave the room while you do that."

We all stepped into the next room while Jean-Claude fiddled with the security system. He punched the keys, placed his thumb on the keypad, then hit the memory button.

Avery glared at me. "What exactly are your qualifications?"

"He knows a thing or two," JD assured.

Her pretty brown eyes flicked to him and filled with disdain.

"And who are you?"

Jack smiled and reintroduced himself.

She was unimpressed.

"We're all set," Jean-Claude shouted.

We entered the gallery again.

Jean-Claude placed his thumb against the keypad, and the lock released. He lifted the glass, then set it back down. After a momentary delay, the case locked again.

Avery put her thumb on the pad, but it didn't work. She punched in her code, and that didn't work either. She smiled with pride. "As it stands, Jean-Claude is the only one who can access this case. Do you feel comfortable with our security measures?"

Jean-Claude surveyed the case for a long moment, then looked at me. "What is your specific concern?"

"There are two relays in that keypad. One for the tamper-resistant sensor and one for the biometric access and keypad. Both of those can be tripped externally without a code."

"How?"

"The keypad is magnetically shielded," Avery interjected. "If Deputy Wild thinks he can run a neodymium magnet alongside the relay and trip the release, he's sadly mistaken." She smiled proudly. "I can demonstrate if you'd like. We have neodymium magnets for sale in the gift shop."

Avery nodded to one of the security guards. He left the gallery and returned a few minutes later with a package of high-powered magnets. He handed them to Avery, and she opened the package and tossed a magnet to me. "In under 30 seconds," she challenged.

I ran the magnet all along the edge of the keypad, hoping to trip the relay. It was usually a simple procedure, but it didn't work. Perhaps she was right. Perhaps the shielding protected the relay. Or the magnet wasn't strong enough.

"Looks like I still have my job," she said with a smug grin. Her eyes flicked to Jean-Claude. "Satisfied?"

He was silent for a moment. "I believe so."

He pressed his thumb against the biometric pad, and the case released. He lifted the glass, and I fished the jewel from my pocket and set it atop the stand.

Jean-Claude sealed the case.

Once it was locked, he gave another tug on the glass for good measure.

Avery smiled. "Don't worry, your precious gem is safe with us."

She nodded to a security guard who wiped the fingerprints from the glass.

"If anybody attempts to tamper with this case, my people will be all over them before they can even think about getting it open," Avery said.

We left the gallery and stepped into the hallway. Avery clicked a button on a key fob, and steel doors embedded within the door frame slid shut, sealing the room. It was like something out of a science fiction movie.

The sound reverberated throughout the cavernous museum.

"You have nothing to worry about," she assured Jean-Claude. "The Jewel of Aphrodite is secure."

## 17

"**I** can't thank you, gentlemen, enough for making this transfer successful," Jean-Claude said as we hovered in the lobby near the museum entrance.

I scanned the parking lot for threats, then escorted Jean-Claude to the car.

"We didn't really do anything," I said. "Your decoys took all the risk. They deserve all the credit."

"Of course."

"And you're comfortable with the security at the museum?" I asked.

Jean-Claude shrugged. "At some point, you have to trust in the Universe. That trust has gotten me this far. I've done everything within my power to secure the stone, short of burying it in a vault forever, which I feel would be a great disservice to humanity. The security seems sufficient, though you seem to think otherwise."

"The men who attacked your decoy today could return to the museum and make another attempt."

"The armed guards will be a deterrent."

"No offense, but those guards wouldn't deter me."

"How would you steal the jewel?"

I thought for a moment. "The human element is always the weakest link. I'd bribe someone on the inside."

"Avery has assured me the security staff has been thoroughly vetted, and I've done my homework as well."

"Everyone has a price."

"Do you have a price?"

"I'm not in this for the money."

"That's part of the reason I chose you two." He paused. "The best defense is a good offense. Devise a plot to steal the jewel. That way, we'll be one step ahead of the thieves."

"I'm sure I can come up with something."

"I have no doubt."

"Do you have any idea who those attackers were?"

"Not Lily Lovelace. It's not her style. She's sly and cunning. It could be Charles Le Grand. But that was a little aggressive for him. I'm not ruling him out, however."

He hopped into the Devastator, and JD drove Jean-Claude to the *Seven Seas*. It was a luxury resort on the beach.

Jack pulled to the passenger drop-off area.

I pulled in behind them and kept my head on a swivel.

Jean-Claude hopped out, and I escorted him into the lobby and transferred him into the care of his security staff. He was their responsibility now.

Damon and crew didn't look any worse for wear, despite the ordeal.

"Thanks again," Jean-Claude said, offering his hand. "I'll be in touch."

His security team escorted him to his room, and I returned to the Devastator. JD waited behind the wheel, under the carport.

"Think the jewel is safe?" JD asked as I leaned into the open passenger window.

"Time will tell."

I followed him to the station. We talked to the sheriff in his office. He sat behind his desk with an annoyed look on his face. "We found the SUVs abandoned on Pompano Drive. The vehicles had been torched."

"These guys are pros," I said.

"Any leads?"

"Not at the moment."

"And this was a private client you took on?"

I nodded.

"Why didn't you tell me beforehand?"

"The client wanted to keep this under the radar. And you know how things have a way of leaking around here."

The sheriff frowned. "And you didn't think I could keep my mouth shut?"

"That's not what I said."

It took a lot to get through the sheriff's thick skin, but I could tell that bothered him. We'd all formed an unspoken bond.

He sighed. "All this for a rock."

"It looks really pretty," JD said.

Daniels gave him a look.

Denise knocked on the door and poked her head in. "I hope I'm not interrupting, but the lab analysis came back. Chocolate was poisoned with strychnine. I thought that stuff was banned."

"You can still get it in gopher bait," Daniels said. "It's allowed for below-ground uses only. Besides, in this day and age, you can get just about anything you want off the Internet." He paused. "Look through the credit card receipts. See if the husband made any purchases recently."

"I'm on it."

"You didn't eat any, did you?" I asked Denise.

"No, I tossed it. And you owe me another box when this is all over."

I chuckled. "I thought you didn't need the sugar."

"I changed my mind." She smiled.

The sheriff's steely eyes took aim at us. "Get over to the store where the husband says he bought the chocolate. Look through the security footage. Let's hope this was an isolated incident. I don't even want to think about some sicko poisoning random candy on store shelves."

As I stood up and left the office, Daniels said, "Next time, keep me in the loop."

---

## 18

**B**eeps and *bloops* filled the air as checkers scanned items across red lasers. Sackers bagged groceries and helped customers to their cars. The smell of fresh java wafted from the in-house coffee shop, mixed with the scents of the floral department.

Coconut Grocery was an upscale mart with fine meats, cheeses, an in-house rotisserie, and rows and rows of packaged goods. Black domed security cameras hung from the ceiling.

We talked to the general manager, Curtis James, about the situation. He'd already pulled that brand of chocolate from the shelves, but others were still available for purchase.

"I assume all transactions are stored in your computer?" I asked.

He nodded.

"I'd like to know the date and time Garrett Clark purchased the chocolate."

"Certainly."

He escorted us to the courtesy counter, commandeered the terminal from an employee, and looked up the information. After a moment of scanning, Curtis said, "Looks like he purchased those yesterday at 12:32 PM."

We asked if we could look at the footage, and he escorted us back to the security room. Monitors hung on the walls with multiple views of all 36 aisles. It was a staggering amount of footage, and one guy was in charge of it all.

"We keep footage for 30 days," Curtis said.

He loaded the footage from 12:32 PM yesterday and scrolled backward until we saw Garrett pull a box of Valentines' chocolate from the shelf and put it in his cart.

"Keep scrolling back," I said.

The footage ran backward at high speed. We watched people race through the store backwards. A few hours earlier in the timeline, a store clerk placed a box of chocolates on the shelf and walked away.

"Stop right there," I said. "Who is that?"

"That looks like Randy." Concern twisted on Curtis's face. "You don't think...?"

I shrugged. "Pull up the returns for that day."

Curtis punched the keys on the computer and searched the transactions. "Looks like a box of chocolate was returned that morning to the courtesy desk and was restocked."

"Who originally purchased the chocolate?" I asked.

Curtis shook his head. "It was a cash transaction."

"Is there a date and time on the receipt?"

He nodded and punched the keys again. "Looks like that was purchased two days before."

"Let's take a look at the footage from that time."

Curtis pulled up the footage. Again we scrolled through it at high speed. We saw two people pull boxes of chocolate from the shelf during that time frame. One was a man that appeared to be in his 60s with graying hair and a round belly. Another was a younger gentleman wearing a full-face motorcycle helmet. It had a black matte base color with a red demon painted on top. It had reptilian eyes facing forward.

The man was fit. Probably somewhere between 25 and 35. The visor was up, but I couldn't see his face. He wore shorts and a T-shirt with a sportbike on the back —an image of a rider taking a corner with a heavy lean angle.

"Pull up other angles. Let's try to follow this guy through the store."

Curtis did as we asked, and we found different views of the suspect walking through the aisles, checking out with the chocolates and nothing else, then exiting.

"We need to find out who that man is," I said. "I need to speak with the clerk at the return counter, the checker, as well as the employee that restocked the chocolate. I'll need copies of the footage."

"No problem."

Curtis punched the keys again and pulled up a receipt for the chocolate, paid for with a credit card in the name of Alan Sullivan. I figured that was the man in his 60s.

I didn't think anyone would be stupid enough to buy chocolate under their own name, poison it, and return it. But stranger things have been known to happen.

Curtis compiled the footage and exported it. I gave him my info, and he emailed it to me and copied Denise and Sheriff Daniels. He also exported a still frame of the suspect, though his face was obscured by a helmet. He texted the image to my phone.

I said to JD, "We need to look into that brand of helmet. That's custom paint. Maybe we can track the purchase."

We left the security room and made our way back to the courtesy counter. We talked to Belinda, who worked the desk yesterday morning. I showed her the image of the moto man, and she didn't really remember the return.

"You have any idea who he is?" I asked.

She shook her head.

"Have you ever seen him in here before?"

She shrugged. "Maybe. I don't know. Sorry I can't be of more help."

We talked to the checker. She had a vague recollection of checking him out. But that was it.

Randy remembered restocking the item, but he never saw the suspect. I took his info and would run his background, but I didn't figure him for any involvement.

Curtis asked, "Do you think any more of the chocolate could be tainted?"

"At this point, we should assume it's all compromised. I'll have the forensic team collect the items you pulled and take samples."

"Okay."

"If you see that man in this store again, call me or the department right away."

"Will do."

We left the store, and I called Denise. "I need you to run background on a gentleman named Alan Sullivan and a stocker named Randy Sims."

"You got it. By the way, I got the footage of the Marco Medina murder. A transportation camera caught part of the incident. I think you'll want to take a look at this."

## 19

The grainy footage played on Denise's monitor as we huddled around her desk. The camera's main focus was a silver Lexus SUV parked by the sidewalk near Taffy Beach. The SUV rocked slightly, and it didn't take a rocket scientist to figure out what was going on behind the steamy windows.

Marco Medina ran into frame chased by Benito Diaz—allegedly. Benito tackled Marco to the concrete. A silver blade glimmered, reflecting a streetlight. Benito stabbed Marco multiple times. Quick strikes like a cobra. Blood blossomed on Marco's shirt. The whole thing happened in the blink of an eye. Benito took off as his victim lay dying. The camera caught a partial view, the action happening at the edge of the frame.

From the footage, there was no way to positively ID Benito. It was too grainy and the camera too far away from the action.

That's where Tara Ward came in.

The silver SUV was registered in her husband's name. But he claimed he wasn't with her that evening. According to Tara's statement, Benito Diaz was the killer, and she ID'd him in a lineup.

"I want to know who was in the vehicle with Tara," I said.

"Obviously not her husband," JD snarked.

"Look through her phone records," I said to Denise. "Let's see if we can find out who she was texting on a regular basis, besides her husband."

"What do you think the odds are Pepe Vasquez will talk to us?" JD asked, knowing the answer.

"Slim to none, but it's worth a shot."

Denise's fingers stroked the keys, pulling up the gang leader's information. "Pepe lives at 915 Harrison Street in Jamaica Village."

JD looked at his watch. "You want to talk to him now?"

"We can try."

I thanked Denise, and we left the Sheriff's Department. I hopped into the Devastator with Jack and left my bike in the lot.

JD twisted the ignition, and the Hemi roared to life. Exhaust growled, and the caged beast was ready to display its might. The car vibrated as the pistons worked their magic. He put the car into gear and rolled out of the lot.

Jamaica Village wasn't exactly a place you wanted to spend much time after dark—or even during daylight hours. There was a lot of gang activity, drugs, and prostitution.

Residents always had to be wary of a stray bullet. Not the best place to raise kids.

We rumbled to the house on Harrison street. It was a dilapidated shotgun shack with peeling white paint and forest green trim. A chain-link fence guarded a gravel driveway, and a low concrete wall ran along the sidewalk.

We parked at the curb, a house down, and hopped out. I gave a cautious glance around as we proceeded toward the home. There were a few kids on bikes near the corner. JD and I pushed through the gate and strolled the walkway to the porch. We climbed the creaky wooden steps and knocked on the door.

A moment later, an older woman shouted through, "Who is it?"

"Coconut County," I said. "We're looking for Pepe Vasquez."

"He doesn't live here."

"You know where we can find him?"

"I don't know anyone by that name."

"Are you sure? DMV records list this as his residence."

"I don't know what to tell you. Your DMV records are wrong."

"What's your name, ma'am?"

"How do I know you're real cops?"

"You can call the Sheriff's Department to confirm our identity if you'd like."

She was silent for a moment. "How about you get off my property?"

I frowned and hesitated. "Sorry to trouble you, ma'am. If you see Pepe, tell him we'll catch up with him sooner or later."

"Like I said. I don't know anyone named Pepe."

We left the porch and walked back toward the car. JD muttered in a skeptical tone, "Think she knows him?"

I shrugged. "Maybe he made up the address. Who knows?"

We hopped into the car, and JD cranked up the engine. He pulled away from the curb, and we rolled up to the kids at the corner. They couldn't have been more than 12 or 13.

With the window down, JD asked, "Do you know where we can find Pepe Vasquez?"

"Who?"

"You know Pepe, right?"

"Never heard of him," the kid said, looking at us with skeptical eyes.

"He doesn't live in that house right there?" JD asked, pointing at the dilapidated rat trap.

"You guys cops?" the kid asked.

"We're just looking for some... you know."

The kids exchanged wary glances, then the leader of the little bikers said, "We don't know anybody named Pepe."

They were lying.

## 20

The kids on the bikes pedaled away, not wanting to talk to us.

JD turned the corner, and we cruised around the neighborhood. It didn't take long to come upon someone dealing on a street corner. We pulled to the curb, and a dude approached the car. He gave a cautious glance in all directions and kept his distance when he asked, "What do you need?"

He was just a kid. Maybe 19, tops.

"Need to find Pepe. You seen him?"

The dealer looked us up and down.

"Nah, man. I ain't seen shit."

"Know where we might be able to find him?"

"No. I don't know anybody by that name."

He backed away from the car and tried to act casual.

A lot of the street dealers had taken to storing drugs in tiny balloons. They'd stuff them in their cheeks and swallow them in case of emergency. They never carried too many on them at any given moment. Usually just enough to stay under the legal threshold for dealing. A stash house was usually nearby. They'd sell all they could hold, then go back for more. In the event of a shakedown, they'd swallow the balloons, obscuring the evidence. Of course, they'd wait around a day or two until it came out the other end and hope the balloons didn't rupture.

I always had a hard time wrapping my head around the fact that people paid good money for questionable product, not knowing where it had been.

Jack pulled away from the corner. Through the side mirror, I saw the dealer pull a cell phone from his pocket and make a call. I had no doubt word was getting around that two cops were looking for Pepe Vasquez.

It was probably a futile effort. The gang leader wouldn't talk to us, even if we found him.

The sun plummeted toward the horizon, and Jack headed toward Oyster Avenue. It was happy hour, and it was our sworn duty to support local businesses.

At the next stoplight, an old Impala pulled up next to us. The car had seen better days. It looked like an old county vehicle—the graphics long since stripped away, leaving a residue and paint discoloration. The white paint was dull and bare in spots. It had a gray primed quarter panel in the front and lots of Bondo on the rear quarter-panel.

There were three guys in the car—two up front and one in the back seat.

The front passenger and the dude in the back pulled out Uzis and opened fire.

Muzzle flash flickered, and smoke wafted from the barrels.

JD and I ducked below the doors as bullets snapped overhead.

The copper rounds plunked into the side of the vehicle.

The windshield webbed with cracks, but the bulletproof glass caught the slugs.

I drew my pistol, waiting for an opportunity to return fire.

The two thugs emptied their magazines in no time, filling the air with a deafening rattle and a cloudy haze.

Tires squealed, and the Impala roared through the intersection.

Horns honked, and tires screeched to avoid collision.

"You okay?" I asked as the smoke cleared.

JD looked himself over and nodded. "Money well spent."

I agreed. The car had kept us safe this time.

I looked myself over to make sure I wasn't hit. My heart thumped, and adrenaline coursed through my veins.

The Impala squealed as it rounded a corner and disappeared.

"You get a plate number?" JD asked.

"No plates on the car. But I remember the shooter's face."

"I'm beginning to think somebody doesn't like us asking around for Pepe," JD said.

"I think you're right."

There was no point in giving chase. The Impala was long gone.

I called Daniels and told him about the shooting. We drove back to the station and examined the car in the parking lot for damage. There were 30+ holes in the side of the Devastator. All the bullets had been stopped by the reinforcements, so they never entered the cabin.

The Plumb Crazy paint was no longer pristine.

"Adds character, don't you think?" I said dryly.

JD surveyed the holes with a frown but finally shrugged with acceptance. "I guess it kind of does."

We pushed inside, and Daniels greeted us. "Making friends as usual, I see."

We shrugged innocently.

"You think these were Pepe's guys?"

"That's a good bet," I said. "I think we rattled their cage."

"And you like them for the Frisky Kitty shooting?"

"With Tara Ward out of the way, Benito walks free."

Daniels had the forensic team pull slugs from the Devastator and run ballistics.

We made our way to the main office and joined Denise at her desk. With a few keystrokes, she pulled up mugshots for

Alonzo Ramirez and Jorge Medina, members of the *Disciples of Hell*.

Pepe's underlings.

Alonzo was a thick, stocky guy with short dark hair, soulless brown eyes, and a mustache. Monochrome tattoos climbed up his neck and sleeved his arms.

Jorge was shaved bald and had similar gang tattoos. He was a little taller and skinnier. Without a doubt, these were the two shooters in the Impala. I didn't get a good look at the driver. For all I know, it could have been Pepe himself.

"I'll get a warrant," Daniels said.

Getting the warrant was easy. Finding the dirtbags was another story.

## 21

Neither of the last known addresses for Alonzo and Jorge were valid. They didn't have cell phones listed in their names and were probably using prepaid burners. We had no way to track these guys down.

I had Denise look up their arrest records. They had quite the storied careers.

"Here you go," she said, looking at her computer screen. "Lena Rivers. 3402 Bowfin Court. She got arrested for DUI, and guess who was with her? Alonzo Ramirez. He was arrested at that time for resisting arrest and battery of an officer. Nice guy. He was also arrested at the Bowfin address for domestic assault."

"Looks like they are living together," I said.

"Could be."

We got an updated warrant from Judge Echols. The charges against him had been dropped, and he was back on the bench. The corruption in this town ran deeper than I thought. It made things awkward, to say the least. But he seemed more agreeable than he previously was.

We suited up in tactical gear and headed to Lena Rivers's residence with Erickson, Faulkner, Mendoza, and Robinson.

She lived in a wheat-colored one story with a grungy 5-foot perimeter wall that enclosed the courtyard. There was a red brick walkway and drive. Palm trees ensconced the home.

With our weapons at the ready, we advanced to the front door. Mendoza and Robinson rounded the house to cover the rear exit. When they were in position, I banged on the front door. "Coconut County! We have a warrant."

We waited a moment.

Lena peered out of the window.

"Movement inside," Faulkner shouted.

"Open up now!" I commanded.

"What do you want?" Lena shouted through the door.

"Open the door, or we're breaking it down."

"Break it down, mother fucker!"

I nodded to Erickson. He and Faulkner heaved the battering ram against the door. It flung wide, splintering shards of wood. We stormed into the house with weapons in the firing position.

Lena stood in the foyer, stunned.

"Down on the ground," I shouted. "Now!"

"Fuck you."

"Get down! Put your hands behind your head."

"I didn't do nothing."

Erickson drew a yellow and black single shot Taser and squeezed the trigger. The blast doors opened, and it struck like a snake. With a 21-foot range, the X92 gave Lena a painful introduction to 50,000 volts at 2.6 milliamps.

She was on the ground, twitching and convulsing in no time.

Faulkner slapped the cuffs around her wrists, and we advanced into the living room, holding up at the entrance to a hallway that led to the bedrooms.

It was a dump inside.

Dishes piled up in the sink. Empty beer bottles and drug paraphernalia on the coffee table. The ashtray was filled with cigarette butts. A glass pipe, thick with tarry residue lay nearby. The place had that faint chemical smell of acetone, reminiscent of methamphetamine.

Lena's face was sunken and drawn. A few of her teeth had decided to go AWOL. Her face was pocked with sores. There was no doubt she had an affinity for the pipe.

We cautiously advanced down the hallway, clearing the guest bathroom on the left and a guest bedroom on the right.

The walls were stained and dirty. The bed was a horror show, and trash littered the floor. The carpet was stained and burned from someone putting out cigarettes. In the closet, we found several weapons—a sawed-off shotgun, an AR 15, a few pistols. A kilo of crystal meth was hidden in a shoebox on a shelf.

We cleared the room and moved on to the master bedroom, holding up at the door. We took a position on either side. Adrenaline flooded my veins. Nothing more ripe with possibilities than a closed door.

I nodded to JD.

He twisted the handle and shoved it open.

We angled our weapons into the room, expecting to find Alonzo, but the bedroom was empty.

We advanced inside, cleared the corners, and searched the master bath. The rest of the house was bad, but this bathroom made the worst truck stop on the highway look clean.

We returned to the living room.

Lena sat on the couch, her wrists cuffed behind her back. "I told you he wasn't here."

"You could have opened the door and said so."

"Who's going to fix that? I'm not paying for it."

I groaned. "Where is he?"

"I don't know."

"When was the last time you saw him?"

"I don't know."

"So the meth in the closet is yours?"

Her face tightened. "That ain't mine."

"Whose is it?"

## 22

The rotors of Tango One thumped overhead, circling the area.

"Where is Alonzo?" I asked.

"I told you," Lena said. "I don't know."

"If you want to go down for everything that's in this house, be my guest. But you're gonna be looking at a long stretch."

She looked at me with terrified eyes.

"Is he still living here?"

She nodded.

"What about Jorge?"

"He sleeps in the guest bedroom."

"Where's Pepe?"

"I don't know."

I gave her a look.

"I swear. I don't know. He doesn't live here. He picked them up earlier."

Tango One crackled over Erickson's radio. "Be advised, we have an inbound Impala heading your way."

"Roger that," Erickson replied.

The minute the thugs saw patrol cars in front of Lena's house, they'd take off.

Faulkner and Mendoza rushed to their respective vehicles while Erickson and Robinson stayed behind. We raced outside with the deputies toward the Devastator.

We weren't fast enough, and the Impala screeched to a halt as it rounded the corner. The driver contemplated throwing it in reverse, but patrol units approached from either side on Birchwood Lane.

I got a good look at him. It was Pepe. No doubt. The other two thugs were with him.

He punched it, and tires squealed. Smoke filled the wheel wells, and the Impala took off down Bowfin, racing past us and the patrol cars.

JD hopped behind the wheel, cranked up the engine, and mashed the pedal to the floorboard. The engine growled, and the exhaust rattled.

It was *snap-your-neck* fast.

We flew down the street, racing past parked cars, picket fences, and trash cans.

The Impala banked a hard left at the next street, and we followed.

Tires squealed again. The suspension was tight, but the added weight of the bullet-proofing didn't help matters. The car fishtailed, and JD counter-steered, bringing it back in line. He was used to the dynamics of the rear-engined Porsche as opposed to the front-heavy muscle car.

The Impala put distance between us, and the patrol units were right behind us, sirens blazing, lights spinning.

The thugs took a hard right on Haven Hearst and barreled down the road. Pepe crossed the dotted yellow line, swerving around a slower vehicle.

We got stuck behind the car, waiting on traffic.

When the lane cleared, JD hammered the pedal again and veered around the car. We raced past the slower car, then swerved in front of it, avoiding oncoming traffic.

The road curved, and the dotted yellow lines became two solid lines.

We gained on them as a truck blocked the Impala. Pepe veered around it, narrowly missing a collision with a midnight blue sedan.

The Devastator rocked and rolled as we took the corners, testing the limits of grip. We swerved around the truck, getting in front of it.

The car was a beast, but it lacked the precision of the Porsche. And all that added weight came with a price.

Tango One pattered overhead, keeping an eye on things. These perps weren't getting away.

The road dog-legged right, and the Impala crossed the dotted yellow lines again to veer around another slower vehicle.

But there was an oncoming truck in the lane.

Horns honked.

The thugs veered right to avoid collision.

Tires squealed.

The truck's bumper clipped the rear quarter panel of the Impala, sending them into a spin.

Metal crumpled, and taillights shattered.

Plastic and glass bounced on the roadway.

The Impala spiraled, leaving black rubber marks across the asphalt. The car slid sideways into a telephone pole, crinkling around the passenger door.

Pepe hopped out and bolted across Haven Hurst, dodging traffic.

From the backseat, Jorge jumped out and sprinted in the opposite direction.

Pepe ran southwest, darted up the driveway of a nearby home, pushed through the gate and into the backyard.

That's when I lost sight of him.

Jorge headed northeast, disappearing into the backyard of a neighboring home as well.

We pulled to the wreckage.

Patrol cars screeched to a halt.

Faulkner and Mendoza hopped out of their vehicles with weapons drawn and advanced toward the Impala.

Alonzo struggled to get out of the car. The telephone pole was taking up half of the passenger seat, and I had no doubt the thug had suffered a broken leg or worse.

He groaned in agony as he tried to get out of the car, but the deputies were there to greet him as he neared the driver's-side door.

I hopped out of the Devastator and gave chase after Jorge. I sprinted up the driveway and pushed through the gate into the backyard.

Jorge sprinted across the patio, around the pool, dodging lounge chairs. There wasn't anywhere for him to run. The house backed up to a canal.

Two girls sunning themselves by the pool shrieked with terror. Their toned bodies glistened in the sun, and pop music blasted from a wireless speaker. Half-empty piña coladas rested on a nearby table.

Palm trees swayed in the breeze, and the teal water of the canal sparkled.

Jorge drew a pistol from his waistband, grabbed the blonde by the arm and yanked her from the lounge chair. With the gun to her head, he took cover behind her oiled body.

Her brunette friend continued to scream, paralyzed with fear.

"Don't come any closer, or I'll fucking kill her, man!" Jorge shouted.

## 23

The rotors of Tango One thumped overhead.

The brunette's ear-piercing shrieks continued, much to the annoyance of Jorge.

"Shut up, bitch, or I will fucking shoot you!"

That didn't exactly help. She tried to stifle her cries, which became whimpers. Tears streamed down her cheeks, running her mascara. She looked like she was about to hyperventilate.

Jorge's wide eyes scanned the area, looking for an escape. He glanced at the helicopter above, then down to the private dock. There was a boat and a *SeaCycle™*.

Jorge was a cornered animal, and cornered animals are dangerous.

"How do you see this all working out?" I asked.

"Back off, or she dies."

I kept my weapon aimed at his head, but I wasn't going to risk the girl. "Seems like you're having a real bad day, Jorge. Let me help you out before it gets worse."

"You want to help me? Put your gun down and walk away. Tell that helicopter to disappear. If it's not gone in 10 seconds, I'm gonna blow her head off."

Both girls shrieked.

Tears rolled down the blonde's cheek. She held still, her body tense.

Her father saw the commotion from inside and stepped onto the patio. The last thing I needed was him doing anything stupid.

"Please," he begged. "I'll give you whatever you want. Just don't hurt my daughter."

"The keys to the boat," Jorge shouted, spotting it at the dock.

"They're inside. I'll be right back. Don't do anything rash."

"Don't tell me what to do!"

The frazzled man darted back inside.

Jorge glanced up at the helicopter for an instant, then his eyes flicked to me. "10 seconds, Pig."

"I don't have a radio. How do you want me to get in touch with them?"

"That's not my problem."

I waved Tango One away.

A moment later, the helicopter banked away but didn't leave the area. But I'm sure it made Jorge feel less smothered.

The girl's father returned with the keys to the boat. He stood across the pool from Jorge and held out the keys. "Here they are. Let her go, and I'll toss the keys to you."

"You don't set the terms," Jorge shouted. "I set the terms."

"Okay. Okay. Whatever you say."

"Go to the boat and start it up."

The man hesitated. I don't think that's what he had in mind.

"Now!" Jorge demanded.

The girl's father looked at me with nervous eyes, then scurried around the pool. He rushed past Jorge and shuffled down the dock. He climbed aboard the 25-foot center-console and cranked up the two outboards.

"Have you thought about where you're going to go, Jorge?" I asked. "How far can you run?"

"As far as I have to."

He started backing toward the dock, still hanging onto Blondie, his pistol against her temple.

"I know you probably think I'm trying to trip you up. But would it be totally outrageous for you to leave the girl on the dock and get into the boat by yourself?"

Asking people for a *no* is easier than asking for a *yes*. Saying yes means obligating yourself to a commitment. Saying *no* is a dismissal. A pre- programmed response.

Jorge didn't answer. He just backed down the dock, glancing from the boat, to the sky, to me. Unfortunately, he didn't take my suggestion. He forced the blonde onto the boat, then demanded the girl's father cast off the lines and render his services as a getaway driver.

I followed cautiously down the dock.

Jorge kept his finger tight around the trigger, continuing to shield himself with the blonde.

"Go!" he shouted to the girl's father.

The blonde's father took the helm, throttled up, and pulled away from the dock. The twin outboards spit white water, creating a helluva wake in the *no wake zone*.

Tango One thumped overhead, giving chase.

The girl's father had done something smart. I spotted a key on the dock he left behind. I snatched it, climbed aboard the *SeaCycle*, cast off the lines, and cranked up the engine. I twisted throttle and cruised through the canal, opening it up when I cleared the *no wake zone*.

The engine howled and left a frothy trail. The *SeaCycle* bounced on the chop, spraying saltwater.

The wind whipped through my hair as I reeled in the center-console boat. But I wasn't sure what the hell I'd do when I caught up to them. Trying to negotiate the release of two hostages from a *SeaCycle* traveling at high speed wasn't necessarily the ideal scenario. And this guy wasn't in the mood to talk.

## 24

A s I drew closer, Jorge took notice.

The center console boat carved through the swells with the girl's father at the helm and Jorge near the stern with the blonde.

When I got close enough to see the anger on his face, Jorge took aim and fired two shots in my direction. The muzzle flashed, and bullets snapped across the water. He was unlikely to hit anything with the boat bouncing on the swells.

The bullets plunked into the water, and I kept on the throttle.

With Jorge distracted, the girl's father took the opportunity to pull a flare gun from a compartment by the helm. He aimed the weapon and squeezed the trigger.

A 12-gauge flare rocketed from the orange gun and pelted Jorge in the back. At short range, it was enough to penetrate the skin. Jorge arched around the impact. Agony twisted on his face.

At several thousand degrees, the tip of the flare burned in his thoracic cavity. Jorge spun around and dove into the water, hoping to extinguish the burning magnesium embedded within him. But nothing would snuff out the flare until it had burned through its fuel source.

Jorge's day went from bad to worse.

The center console circled around as Jorge flailed in the water, slapping at the surface.

By the time I reached him, he'd lost the fight with the flare and submerged below the surface.

I cut the throttle and dove into the water after him. Jorge's limp body sank as I swam through the water.

I pulled him to the surface, and the center console pulled alongside. The girl's father wasn't too eager to render aid to the man who had just taken his daughter hostage, but he grabbed hold of Jorge's wrist and pulled him onto the boat with my assistance. I climbed aboard, dripping wet.

The blonde trembled, thoroughly shaken by the experience.

Jorge was gone, and there was no bringing him back.

"Who is he?" the girl's father asked as he stood over the body.

The man embraced his shaking daughter, and they squeezed each other tight as I told them the story.

The smell of Jorge's burned flesh drifted about the cockpit. He'd been cooked from the inside out.

Tango One circled overhead along with a news helicopter, and we were soon surrounded by patrol boats.

Ted Travers was the man's name, and his daughter was Britney. Ted followed the patrol boats back to the station. Brenda greeted us on the dock with her crew, and Jorge was transferred into her custody for examination.

Ted and Britney gave a statement and filled out reports. No charges would be brought against Ted.

JD met me at the station, and we filled out after-action reports. Faulkner and Mendoza had taken Alonzo into custody, and he'd been rushed to the emergency room and treated. He had a broken femur, several cracked ribs, and some pretty severe bruising.

I followed Jack on my bike to the hospital. We made our way through the sea-foam green hallways of the trauma center. The sound of ventilators spilled from dim rooms. Nurses checked on patients. The air smelled sterile and dirty at the same time. The temperature was always freezing.

Alonzo had a semi-private room. He lay in bed, his leg in a cast. A heart monitor blipped bedside, and the TV mounted on the wall was off. I had called the hospital and asked that he be sequestered from the news. I didn't want him to know that Jorge was dead.

Alonzo's face twisted into a scowl when he saw us. His left wrist was cuffed to the bedrail.

"Looks like they've got you all fixed up," I said with a grin.

"I ain't saying shit to you."

"That's okay. You don't have to."

A quizzical look played on his face.

"Your buddy, Jorge, spilled the beans. He's trying to save his ass. So you can lay there and remain silent, and this whole thing is going to come down on you."

His eyes narrowed at me.

"Look, you're already in deep for the attempted murder of two police officers." I pointed between JD and myself. "Jorge says you killed Tara Ward. He says you're the one who marched into the Frisky Kitty and started plugging the patrons full of holes."

His face twisted. "What are you talking about?"

"I get it. You were trying to save your friend. But Benito is beyond saving." That wasn't exactly the truth. The punk was most likely going to walk.

Jorge laughed.

"Is this funny?"

"Yeah, it's funny because you don't know what the fuck you're talking about."

"Are you telling me that Jorge is making it all up?"

"I know Jorge, and he's no rat. Nice try, Pig."

"You're trying to tell me you weren't the active shooter? You better give me something compelling."

"I don't know where you get your information from, but I didn't have anything to do with that shooting. And I'm not gonna take the fall for that shit."

"You're gonna do a long stretch for attempted murder. Might as well admit to the shooting. I can talk to the state attorney. If you cooperate and save the state a trial, maybe you can get a better deal."

"Fuck you."

I smiled. "Enjoy life in prison."

I nudged JD, and we stepped out of the room. I waved to the nurse at the station as we headed down the hallway toward the elevator.

"Think he knows anything?" JD asked.

"Tara Ward's death gets Benito off the hook. She sure as hell didn't shoot herself. I'm pretty sure Pepe and his crew were involved somehow."

A BOLO was out for Pepe. Alonzo was looking at life, and Jorge had lost his. I hoped we'd have the ringleader in custody soon.

My stomach rumbled. It had been a long day. We left the hospital, and I followed JD as he drove the Devastator back to the marina. I took a shower and washed off the saltwater, changed clothes, and we stopped in *Diver Down* for a drink and something to eat.

Teagan greeted us with that bubbly smile of hers.

I filled her in on the events of the day as I chowed on the pink shrimp, sautéed with fresh basil and a red chili glaze over creamy risotto. Jack had the black grouper with shrimp and lobster sauce with sautéed spinach.

We were halfway through the meal when Denise called. "I've got bad news."

## 25

"**A**nother woman died," Denise said. "Brenda's at the scene now. Daniels wants you to get over there."

"What happened?"

"That's what you two are supposed to figure out."

"We're on it," I said before ending the call.

I informed JD.

"No rest for the weary. Hurry up, and let's roll."

We shoveled the last bites in our mouths and hustled out of the bar. We cruised the Devastator to 746 Golden Eagle Way. Red and blues swirled from patrol cars. Curious neighbors peered through blinds and loitered on the street.

We parked the car, hustled up a walkway to the front door, and pushed inside. It was a nice pastel-yellow one-story with a wide driveway that was home to a sporty mid-sized white SUV. The house was shrouded by trees. A brown, solid board gothic fence enclosed the property.

Camera flashes filled the living room as Dietrich snapped photos. Brenda hovered over the body. A teary-eyed woman stood nearby, watching the scene in horror.

The open box of Valentine's chocolates on the glass coffee table gave me an indication of what we were dealing with. The brand was different, but it was a similar style of candy —chocolate squares stuffed in the middle with all kinds of creamy, gooey goodness. Perhaps, even something a little sinister.

"Her name is Melinda Dandridge," Brenda said. "No signs of trauma."

Melinda lay slumped on the beige cloth couch, one arm hanging off. She was late 30s with golden-brown hair, and a little fuller-figure than she would have liked—round, chubby cheeks and a small double chin. A turquoise necklace dangled around her collarbone. Her brown eyes gazed into the void. Her skin was pale, her lips blue. She looked like she'd suffocated. Strychnine has a nasty side effect of muscle paralysis, rendering the victim unable to breathe.

"And who are you?" I asked the teary woman.

"I'm Christy Epps. I'm a friend. Melinda called last night and said she wasn't feeling well. I called this morning to check on her but didn't get an answer. I kept calling all day and finally decided to stop by. She didn't answer the door, so I used my spare key." She broke into sobs. "I found her like this on the couch."

Tears sprayed, and her chest heaved and jerked.

Christy was 36-ish with dyed auburn hair, blue eyes, heavy liner, and a petite little figure. By the looks of things, regular Botox injections kept the wrinkles in her forehead away. She looked like she spent a good amount of time at the gym.

I hovered over the coffee table, examining the chocolates. "You know when she purchased these?"

Christy shook her head.

"Let's have these analyzed," I said to Brenda. "Do you have a time of death?"

"According to the body temperature, I'd put it between 2 and 4 AM this morning."

"What time did you talk to her?" I asked Christy.

"It was maybe 10 or 10:30 PM. I asked her if she wanted me to come over or if she needed anything. She said that she'd be fine. She thought it was maybe something she ate. I told her to go to the ER if she thought she really needed help. She was always a little stubborn when it came to her health."

"And she lives here alone?"

Christy nodded.

"Was she dating?"

"Not currently. She broke up with her boyfriend last year. She was still hung up on him. She hadn't quite gotten over it yet. It was a pretty nasty breakup."

"Was she depressed?"

"I don't think she was thrilled about being single this time of year. Valentine's Day is great when you're in a relationship. Not so much when you're not."

I didn't really think that Melinda had committed suicide by chocolate, but we needed to keep all possibilities open.

JD and I searched the house, and we found a receipt from Sunset Grocery for the purchase of the chocolates. I called the store, spoke with the manager, and told him to pull this brand of chocolate from the shelf. "Might as well pull all brands," I said.

He wasn't happy about it, but he agreed to do it. It was better than the impending lawsuits if multiple people died from contaminated products. I told him to keep the items until the forensic investigators had a chance to collect and analyze them.

Our worst fears were being realized. It seemed this wasn't an isolated incident. We had a serial poisoner on our hands. To make it worse, there was no obvious motive and no intentional target. It's hard to narrow down suspects with no connection to their victims. It's why traveling serial killers can go decades without apprehension. Most people are killed by someone they know. Crimes of passion.

We wrapped up at the scene and filled out a report at the station, then JD dropped me off at the marina. The next morning, I got a call from Agent Kelso with the DEA.

More bad news.

## 26

Kelso wasn't happy. "I saw that you took down two of Pepe's gang."

"What's your interest?" I asked.

"My interest is that I've been having a CI make *buys* from them for the last six months, trying to get to their supplier. Pepe is small time. I want the big fish. Thanks to you, that's not going to happen now."

"There's a good chance those guys are responsible for the Frisky Kitty shooting."

"No. There's no chance."

I groaned, knowing where this was going. "Why do you say that?"

"Because my CI was making a *buy* from them during the same time as the shooting."

I grimaced. "You sure about that?"

"I'm positive."

"And all three of them were present during the *buy*?"

"Yes."

"Can you trust your informant?"

"I don't have to trust my informant. I have video and audio."

A frustrated breath escaped my lungs. "Well, that sucks."

"It sure does."

I didn't really appreciate his accusatory tone. "What do you want me to do about it?"

"Maybe you guys shouldn't go off half-cocked."

"Maybe you guys ought to communicate better with the Sheriff's Department about your investigations."

Kelso grumbled something about operational security and hung up. Guess he didn't like my tone either.

I pulled myself out of bed, showered, fixed breakfast, and called JD. I told him we were back to square one with the Frisky Kitty shooting. It was time to take another look at the victims and see what we missed.

JD picked me up in the Porsche, and we drove to Sunset Grocery and spoke with Carl, the manager. He'd pulled all of the Valentine's Day candy from the shelves. We looked up the returns, and sure enough, a box had been brought back to the courtesy counter the day before, un-opened. A replay of the security camera footage from the time showed the same man, wearing the demon motorcycle helmet, making the return.

There was no way to see his face.

Carl exported the footage and sent it to the Sheriff's Department.

We interviewed the staff—nobody remembered the guy.

Daniels had Denise contact every store in Coconut Key and ask them to remove all Valentine's Day candy. I contacted Paris Delaney and asked her to get the word out.

"You want me to tell the audience that all recently purchased chocolate should be thrown out?"

"Or they can drop it off at the Sheriff's Department for evaluation."

"This is big. How many items do you think are tainted?"

"We're looking at two deaths so far and chocolate from two different grocery stores."

"Melinda Dandridge?"

"We don't have official confirmation that she was poisoned yet, but all signs point in that direction."

"I'll get the word out. This is going to cause mass hysteria."

"That's right up your alley," I said dryly. "It'll be a ratings boon."

"It's not all about ratings, Deputy. Sometimes it's about saving lives." There was a hint of sincerity in her tone.

"I'm sure you'll have an up-to-the-minute poison tracker before too long."

"Ooh, that is a good idea. Hopefully, there are no more locations to track," she said before ending the call.

We left Sunset Grocery and drove to Ray's Cycle Universe. I had purchased a few sportbikes from Ray, and he always took care of me.

The bell chimed as we pushed inside the pristine showroom. It smelled like fresh rubber and steel. The place was spotless. You could perform surgery in here.

The showroom was filled with everything from the latest crotch rockets to the biggest, baddest, and meanest Harleys on the block. There were racks of clothing, racing leathers, helmets, gloves, and accessories.

Ray greeted us with a smile and a wave. We shook hands across the counter.

"What can I do for you today? Looking to upgrade?"

"I'm already at the top. I don't know where I'd go from here."

"Could be time to start thinking about customization," Ray said, trying to plant the seed in my head.

I chuckled. I didn't need to customize the bike. It was already too fast.

"I pulled out my phone and showed him a picture of the demon motorcycle helmet. "That could be a custom paint job. You recognize the work?"

Ray shook his head. "That's a factory option. You can order these with any number of custom designs. Hell, you can even upload your own design, and they'll print it on the helmet, for a fee, of course."

I frowned. I was hoping it would be a one-off design. "Does that helmet look familiar?"

## 27

"I've seen that design, but I don't recall selling any here, if that's what you're getting at," Ray said. "A lot of people come in here, try on the helmets for size, then go order them online. Maybe they save a few bucks. It is what it is."

I showed him a picture of the T-shirt the killer wore. "You recognize the shirt?"

Ray frowned and shook his head.

I thanked him for the information and shook his hand again before leaving.

"You let me know when you want performance upgrades," he said, calling after us as we pushed out the door.

We hopped into the Porsche and headed across the island to speak with Evan Conroy. Denise had pulled Tara Ward's phone records, and there was an inordinate amount of texts between the two. I was pretty sure he was the other occupant of the SUV the night of Marco Medina's murder. He'd probably seen the whole thing but didn't want to testify due to the fact that he was married and had two kids.

We headed to his office at *Fulbright, Lopez, & Fletcher*. He worked as a bean counter for the high-profile accounting firm. The six-story building was located a few blocks off the beach.

JD pulled into the lot, found a place to park, and we strolled inside. The atrium was full of ferns, and a soothing waterfall trickled. The glass elevator took us to the third floor, where the firm occupied most of the space.

I flashed my badge to the receptionist. "We're here to see Evan Conroy."

Concern bathed her face. She picked up the phone and dialed his extension. "Mr. Conroy, there are two deputies here to see you."

His voice filtered through the speaker in her phone, but I couldn't make out what he said.

"I don't know," the receptionist replied. "They didn't say. You'll have to ask them."

Evan said something else.

"Yes, sir. I'll tell them." She hung up the phone, then looked at us. "He'll be with you shortly. Please, have a seat. Can I get you anything to drink? Water? Soda?"

"No, thank you," I said.

The office was sleek and modern. We took a seat on the leather sofa. Magazines were neatly arranged on the coffee table. The subjects ranged from cars and boats to architecture and current events.

Evan greeted us in the lobby a few minutes later. He was a handsome man in his mid 40s with short salt-and-pepper hair. He wore a nice gray suit and matching tie. He was fit and trim. A forced smile tugged his lips as he extended his hand. "Deputies, what can I do for you?"

"I'm Tyson Wild, and this is Jack Donovan. We'd like to talk you about Tara Ward."

His brow knitted. "Who?"

"I think you might prefer it if we spoke in your office."

He glanced to the receptionist who had been hanging on our every word. Her eyes flicked down to her desk, pretending not to eavesdrop.

Evan swallowed hard and cleared his throat. "Certainly. Right this way."

He escorted us down a hallway, past other offices. He had a corner space with a nice view. Over the tops of neighboring buildings, you could catch a glimpse of the ocean in the distance.

Evan's accreditations hung on the wall in nice frames. There were several pictures of his wife and two children on his desk. Accounting books lined the shelves, and a large flatscreen monitor sat atop his desk. He closed the door behind us as we entered and offered us a seat.

"You can skip the denials," I said. "We know you were with Tara Ward the night of the murder."

His shoulders slumped, and a grim frown tugged his face. He sighed as he sat down. "You have to understand, I'm a family man."

"Clearly," JD said in a sardonic tone.

"I couldn't come forward. My relationship with Tara would be exposed. My wife would be devastated. My family would collapse."

"All things you should have thought about before banging her in her SUV on the seawall," I said.

"You can't prove I was in the vehicle."

"I thought we weren't playing games anymore."

He was silent for a long moment.

"Benito Diaz is going to walk without an eyewitness. I'm here to ask you to come forward and cooperate with the state's attorney to put that guy away."

Torment filled his face. "You're asking me to throw away my marriage?"

"I'm asking you to do the right thing."

"I love my wife."

"That's why you were with Tara in her SUV."

"It's complicated."

"It always is."

He was silent again for a long moment. "Do you know who killed Tara?"

"We have several leads, but none of them are panning out right now. Can you add any insight?"

"I figured it was the same guys that killed Marco Medina."

"So did we. But that proved not to be the case."

He sighed again. "Look. I really want to help you. I do. But I just can't get involved. Besides destroying my family, it would put them in danger. You know how ruthless these people are."

"Two of those gang members are out of the picture. One is still on the run."

"And the one on the run is probably dangerous, is he not?"

I couldn't argue with that.

I dug into my pocket and slid my card across the desk. "Take your time. Think about it. Call me when you decide to do the right thing."

I stood up, thanked him for his time, and we left the office. We smiled and waved at the receptionist as we passed, and I could see the curiosity in her eyes.

In the hallway, JD asked, "Think that guy will man up?"

I shrugged. "Doubtful."

We made our way to the elevator, and JD pressed the call button. It lit up, and a moment later, the bell dinged, and the doors slid open. Just as we were stepping aboard, my phone buzzed with a call from Sheriff Daniels. The doors closed as he began to speak, and the signal dropped as the elevator descended.

## 28

I called the sheriff back when we stepped out of the elevator.

"Your moonlighting gig might be going south," Daniels said.

I clenched my jaw and stifled a groan. "What happened?"

"Get to the museum and find out." There was a hint of amusement in his voice. "Fire alarm went off. I don't think it's a coincidence."

"We're on our way."

I ended the call, and we rushed out of the professional building, hopped into the Porsche, and raced to the museum.

The parking lot was pure chaos.

Patrons had been evacuated. The fire department and EMTs were on the scene. Red and white LEDs flickered, and smoke wafted from the building. Spectators gawked. Fire-fighters wore helmets and full protective gear with respira-tors. A few entered the building to determine the source and status of the blaze.

Paris Delaney and crew were on scene filming the spectacle.

The smoke didn't have the typical acrid stench of most building fires. It was more of a magnesium smell. I recog-nized the scent instantly. This was no accidental fire. It was a decoy to fill the building with smoke and get the patrons out.

The museum had a clean-agent fire suppression system. Water could damage precious works of art. The inert gas of the clean-agent system would flood the room and disrupt the combustion process. Fires would theoretically be extin-guished before they had time to do millions of dollars worth of damage. The gas system required each room to be airtight for maximum effectiveness.

Avery waited in the parking lot with the museum staff and security. Worry crinkled her face.

"Do you know what happened?" I asked.

"There was smoke. The fire alarm went off. People were evacuated. The suppression system was activated auto-matically."

"What about the Jewel of Aphrodite?"

Her face went pale. "What about it?"

I gave her a look.

"Please tell me you've considered the fact that this was all a diversion?"

She stammered, but nothing came out.

I frowned and shook my head. She was a young, inexperienced curator, fresh out of art school, who clearly got the job through connections.

A firefighter exited the smoke-filled building, pulled off his respirator, and spoke with us. "The fire's been extinguished. Looks like it started in a trashcan." He held up a spent smoke canister. "We found several of these in various trash cans."

I pulled on a pair of nitrile gloves that I had in my pocket and examined the canister. "This was on a timer. I'm guessing they were synchronized to go off simultaneously."

Avery's face went long.

My phone buzzed with a call from Jean-Claude. His worried voice filtered through the speaker in my phone. "I just saw the news. Tell me everything's okay?"

"Don't hold your breath."

"Is it safe?"

"I haven't been inside the building yet. I'll report back shortly."

I scanned the parking lot, looking for anyone suspicious. I figured the perps were long gone, but sometimes criminals liked to stick around and watch the show.

The smoke had mostly dissipated, leaving a soupy haze in the air. JD and I borrowed spare respirators from the firefighters and pushed into the museum. We advanced through the fog to the second level, then into the gallery that housed the Jewel of Aphrodite. I cut through the cloudy air. After a few steps, the *impenetrable* case in the center of the room came into view.

## 29

It didn't come as a shock to see that the case was empty.

The jewel was gone.

A quick glance around the room revealed that nothing else was missing.

I exchanged a frustrated glance with JD, and he just shook his head.

We hustled downstairs and stepped outside to rejoin Avery. Her eyes filled with hopeful anticipation.

I shook my head, deflating any optimism that remained. "I'll need to see the security footage."

She looked like she'd seen a ghost. She swallowed hard, and her body trembled. She couldn't move, and she couldn't speak.

"Pull it together," I said.

After a moment, she swallowed and cleared her throat. "It's really gone?"

"Yes, it's really gone."

She processed for a second. "Right this way."

We donned our respirators again, and she borrowed a spare from the fire department. We rushed inside and made our way through the haze to the security office.

Avery hunched over a computer terminal and scrolled through the footage to the moment when the fire started. It had originated in a trashcan on the second floor, just as the fireman suspected. Multiple other trash cans billowed smoke. Haze filled the air, making the camera footage worthless. Then the wireless feed was disrupted completely. It was clear that someone had jammed or disabled the wireless signal.

This was no amateur job.

"Backup before the fire," I said, my voice muffled by the full face mask.

There were multiple screens and dozens of feeds. I scanned the crowd, looking for Charles Le Grand or Lily Lovelace. I had no doubt that whoever was behind this wore a disguise.

I noticed a woman with long curly red hair and dark sunglasses enter the museum. I followed her through different camera angles as she moved through the galleries. She paid scant attention to the master works of art. The hair and the sunglasses did a good job of hiding her face, and she seemed to know how to avoid looking into the cameras. She could have been Lily Lovelace. It was hard to say. Her nose was bigger than in the photo Jean-Claude had sent me. It could have been a prosthetic.

The redhead made a beeline for the gallery upstairs that housed the jewel. I never saw her place anything in the trash cans. It is my suspicion that she placed the smoke grenades earlier in the day or sometime previously. Perhaps someone else placed them for her.

We kept watching the footage. The suspect lingered in a neighboring galley, pretending to admire a painting. Then smoke filled the museum. That's when I lost track of her. It would have been easy for her to dart into the jewel room, acquire the target, and escape with the evacuating crowd. No one would give her a second thought. The security alarms were already blaring.

"Is there any security footage of the parking lot?" I asked.

Avery shook her head. "The stuff we try to protect is inside the museum." She was still in a daze. "I don't understand. How did she get into the case?"

"I told you that case was vulnerable."

"But that's not possible."

"Well, the empty case says otherwise."

She stared at me blankly, her eyes wide, the magnitude of her failure dawning on her. "I'm so screwed."

"Get your résumé together. You might be looking for another job."

## 30

"I'm so sorry, Mr. Juneau," Avery said when Jean-Claude arrived with his entourage. "I take full responsibility."

"It's not your fault. These things happen." He was surprisingly calm when he greeted us on the steps of the museum.

A crowd gathered, and cameras closed in. Reporters shouted questions.

By this time, Sheriff Daniels had joined us.

Jean-Claude ignored the chaos. He was a focused, centered man. Nothing seemed to frazzle him. "Our focus now is to recover the jewel before it leaves the country. I'd like to take a look at the security footage."

"Certainly," Avery said. "Right this way."

She escorted Jean-Claude into the museum, and we followed. By this time, the smoke had cleared, and only the odor remained.

Jean-Claude muttered to me, "You were right. I should have listened."

I didn't gloat.

Avery pulled the footage up on the monitors in the security room, and Jean-Claude reviewed the feeds. I pointed out the woman that I suspected was Lily Lovelace.

Jean-Claude studied the image carefully. "I can't be certain, but that could be her. As I mentioned, she is a master of disguise."

"The sheriff put out a BOLO on the suspect. I've got my resources looking for credit card transactions, cell phone data, or anything else that may allow us to pinpoint her location." I had called Isabella and pulled in another favor, though I doubted Lily would leave any trail behind.

Jean-Claude echoed my thoughts. "Lily Lovelace will be using an alias, that much I can guarantee. As I mentioned previously, Deputy, I'm relatively certain the buyer for this jewel is Anatoly Vetrov. All we have to do is locate him and wait for Lily to attempt an exchange. Your job has shifted from protection to recovery. You can name your price."

"We can discuss that later." It wasn't about the money for me. It never was.

We left the security room and joined the forensic investigators in the second-floor gallery. They dusted the case and keypad for prints, but I doubted they'd find any. Our jewel thief was far too sophisticated to leave prints on the glass or keypad.

The forensic team rounded up all the smoke canisters and dusted them as well.

"How did she get into the case?" Jean-Claude asked.

The case still functioned, and there were no signs of tampering. I gave him several of my theories, but that's all they were—theories.

"The only real evidence we have to go on are the smoke canisters," JD said.

"I'll see if we can track the purchase," Daniels said.

"Good luck with that," I said. "The lot number has been scratched off the canisters. The sale will be hard to track." I paused. "Not to be a pessimist, but our thief isn't an amateur."

"There is no such thing as a perfect crime," Daniels said. "And I have faith that you two will sort this out."

"It's good to see the sheriff has such confidence in you two," Jean-Claude said to us. "Makes me feel better."

The minute we stepped out of the museum, Paris accosted us along with a gaggle of reporters. Camera lenses focused, and several fluffy boom mics hung overhead.

"Can you confirm the Jewel of Aphrodite was stolen?" Paris shouted.

Still cameras flashed.

Reporters pushed and shoved each other for better angles.

Jean-Claude paused, holding court on the steps. "Yes, I can confirm that the jewel was stolen. I'm working with local authorities, and I'm certain the stone will be recovered shortly."

"Do you know who stole it?"

"Was this a lone perpetrator, or was this a group effort?"

"How was the heist carried out?"

The questions came rapid-fire.

Jean-Claude smiled. "I've said all I can at this time. If anyone saw anything suspicious while they were visiting the museum, please contact the authorities."

We escorted Jean-Claude through the crowd to a waiting limousine while reporters continued to shout questions.

Damon opened the rear passenger door.

"Keep me updated, Deputy," Jean-Claude said as he slipped into the cushy leather seats.

Damon closed the door, gave us a dirty look, then hustled into the passenger's seat. The limo slowly pulled away, weaving through the crowd and emergency vehicles.

"That guy's a piece of work," Daniels muttered. "Why bring the damn thing out in public view anyway?"

"That was the idea."

He shook his head. "How does someone so foolish get so rich?"

"I don't know. JD, care to answer that?"

Jack flashed a friendly scowl.

We headed to the station and filled out after-action reports. I texted Isabella and asked her to keep an ear out for any chatter about the jewel.

Denise poked her head into the conference room as we typed away on iPads. "Toxicology report came back. Melinda Dandridge had a lethal amount of strychnine in her system. The chocolates found in her home tested positive. But not every piece. It seems the killer just poisoned a few pieces and called it a day."

"Were there any more boxes of tainted chocolate found?"

"Not yet, but the lab is working their way through tons of chocolate."

"Keep me posted."

"I will," she said with a smile.

We finished up, then headed back to *Diver Down* to grab something to eat. We took a seat at the bar, and Teagan greeted us with a smile.

Harlan sat in his usual seat, sipping on a beer, eating a turkey club sandwich.

Paris Delaney's segment from the museum played on the flatscreen behind the bar. She detailed the mythical story behind the precious jewel, and the segment cut to clips of her interview with Jean-Claude on the museum steps. She wrapped up the segment by saying, "Tune in tonight for part one of my multipart segment on the Jewel of Aphrodite."

She wasn't one to waste an opportunity.

She moved on to the news about the poisoning. "A second victim has been confirmed, and authorities are urging everyone to avoid any recently purchased Valentine's Day chocolates. This is a cowardly act by a depraved individual.

If you're out there, listening, I urge you to come forward and alert authorities to any remaining poisoned items."

She went on to insult the killer, trying to spur a response, I assumed.

"You boys ready for lunch?" Teagan asked.

"You read my mind," JD teased. "I'll take a mushroom cheeseburger."

"And for you?" Teagan asked me.

"The same with a side of sweet potato fries."

"Coming right up." She punched in our order, sending it to the kitchen. Absent-mindedly, she grabbed a piece of chocolate from a box of candy below the counter. She popped the square into her mouth and chewed a mouthful of gooey goodness.

I watched in disbelief. "What are you doing!?"

"Nothing," she said with her mouth full.

"Spit that out!"

Her face crinkled. "This is the box you gave me. I've already eaten half of it, and I'm still alive."

"Doesn't matter. We don't know when this guy started tampering with the candy. I thought you had thrown that out?"

"I didn't think anything about it."

I groaned. "Spit!"

She found a nearby trashcan and emptied the chocolate from her mouth. She grabbed a napkin and wiped her pretty lips. "Those were so good, too."

"Throw the rest of the box out."

"Can't you test it?"

"Throw it out. I will buy you another box after we catch this guy."

"Promise?"

"I promise."

A delightful smile curled on her plump lips.

Then it faded.

Her eyes rounded, and panic bathed her face. It looked like she couldn't breathe.

## 31

M y stomach twisted, and worry tensed my body. My eyes widened. "Are you okay?"

Teagan struggled to inhale a breath.

I launched from the barstool and started to round the bar.

She burst into laughter, not able to sustain the ruse any longer.

My eyes narrowed, and I scowled at her. "That's not funny."

"You were scared." In singsong, she teased, "You care about me."

"Do that again, and I might change my feelings."

She laughed. "Please, you were just excited at the prospect of giving me mouth-to-mouth."

"In your dreams." I'd love to give her mouth-to-mouth.

"I'll give you mouth-to-mouth," Harlan said.

"Harlan, are you healthy enough for cardiopulmonary resuscitation?" Teagan teased.

"Honey, I'm healthy enough for a lot of things," the old Marine said in a lewd tone.

We hung out and talked to Teagan about the heist while we waited for our food. It didn't disappoint when it arrived. We chowed down on the cheeseburgers and filled our bellies, plotting our next move.

My phone buzzed with a call from McKenzie, the new Chief of Staff in Commissioner Johnson's office.

"Deputy Wild?"

"You got him. What can I do for you?"

"I found something concerning."

She had my attention.

"As you know, I took over Crosby's position. Which means I inherited his desk, his office computer, and all his duties. I found some disturbing emails in the deleted files folder. I think you should have a look at these. Is there somewhere we could meet?"

"You can meet us at the station. We're at Diver Down right now. You can come here, or we can come to you. Whatever you prefer."

"I'm on my lunch break. I'll meet you at Diver Down in 15 minutes."

"That sounds great. Tell me what you found in the emails?"

"I made printouts. I'll bring them with me. It looks like Crosby was threatening to go public."

"Public with what?"

"Crosby demanded money from the commissioner," she said in a hushed tone. "It looks like he found out Mr. Johnson was taking payoffs to vote for development deals."

"That could be a motive to kill someone," I said.

"This is frightening." Her voice trembled. "Do you think this is why Crosby was killed?"

"Could be. Where are you now?"

"In my car in the parking lot. I'm heading your way."

"Does anyone else know about this?"

"I haven't told a soul."

She ended the call, and I filled JD in on the situation.

"What a scumbag," he said. "I never liked the commissioner. Didn't vote for him."

We waited for McKenzie's arrival.

And waited...

And waited...

30 minutes went by, and McKenzie still hadn't shown up. I dialed her cell, and it went straight to voicemail.

I called back again—no luck.

That terrible feeling twisted in my gut. I gave a worried look to JD. "She's not picking up."

"Maybe she got stuck in traffic."

I shook my head. Even with traffic, it didn't take 45 minutes to get from City Hall to *Diver Down*. The only time the island saw *that* kind of traffic was during spring break.

I called one more time to no avail, then I dialed Denise. "I was supposed to meet with an informant, but she didn't show up. Have there been any reports of anything unusual?"

"Hang on, I'll check." Her fingers tapped the keys. "There's a traffic accident on the corner of Snook and Mackerel. Hit-and-run. One fatality. Officers are on scene now."

I cringed. "Do you know who the victim's car is registered to?"

Her fingers tapped the keys again. "The report says the vehicle is registered to McKenzie Malloy."

My jaw tensed.

"That's not your informant, is it?"

"Unfortunately."

"Oh, no. I'm so sorry."

"Thanks."

I ended the call and told JD the bad news. We hustled out of the bar, hopped into the Porsche, and zipped across town to the site of the accident.

Shards of glass glittered in the sunlight. The driver's side door of McKenzie's silver Honda Accord was caved in. The vehicle had been T-boned.

There were no tire tracks. It looked like the offending vehicle never hit the brakes.

McKenzie's car was dragged through the intersection and spun around. The airbags had deployed and lay limp like pockets turned out.

First responders had removed McKenzie's body from her vehicle. She lay covered on a yellow gurney. Blood stained the deflated airbags and speckled the interior.

Emergency lights flickered, and traffic was backed up in all directions.

We hopped out and approached Mendoza, who had responded to the initial call.

"Got a witness that saw a truck smash into the silver sedan." He pointed to a guy in his late 20s standing nearby. "Said it was a black Super Duty with tinted windows. Didn't get a look at the driver. Smashed into the little Honda, fullbore. Said it didn't do much to the truck, just busted out the headlights.

"Yeah, the truck plowed through and kept going," the witness said.

"This is Justin," Mendoza said.

We shook hands and made introductions.

Justin had shaggy brown hair that curled into his eyes. He had a narrow face, an angular nose, and a mustache that didn't really fit. It was like he grew it as a joke.

"Anybody get a license plate?" I asked.

"Yeah," Mendoza said. "It comes back stolen."

"Figures," JD muttered.

I poked my head into McKenzie's vehicle and glanced

around. The tinny smell of blood lingered in the air. Shards of glass sparkled on the seats, but I didn't see any printouts of incriminating emails. I looked in the backseat, then popped the trunk. If McKenzie had the emails with her, they weren't here now.

I asked Mendoza, "Has anybody taken anything out of the vehicle?"

"Just the girl," he said, pointing to the gurney.

My face tightened.

"What's the matter?"

"I knew this woman. She was bringing me information."

"I saw somebody," Justin said.

I gave him my full attention.

"Just after the truck took off, a guy on the corner rushed to the car. I thought he was going to check on the girl, but he leaned over her, grabbed her purse and some papers and took off. I couldn't believe it. The guy stole her purse while she was dying. What the hell is the world coming to?"

"Where were you when this went down?"

He pointed to the street corner. "I was right there, waiting for the light to change to cross the street."

"Can you describe the guy that took the purse?"

"Yeah. He was maybe 6-feet tall. Wore a baseball cap and sunglasses. Hawaiian shirt and cargo shorts." He pointed at JD. "Sorta like him, but with short blond hair. Younger." Justin studied Jack carefully. "Hey, you're in that band, right?"

Jack puffed up. "I could be."

"Yeah, I saw you guys at Sonic Temple. Not bad."

I got Justin's contact information and told him a sketch artist from the department would call him. I asked Mendoza if there were any other witnesses. Dozens of people stood around, gawking at the carnage, but nobody came forward. People just didn't want to get involved. They didn't want to take the time off work and get called in to testify in a criminal trial.

I made the grim walk over to the gurney and pulled back the cover and looked at McKenzie's face. It wasn't a pretty sight. Battered and bruised, swollen and bloodied. But it was her. Dario Johnson's new Chief of Staff.

## 32

It was no surprise that Judge Echols denied our request for a warrant. We wanted to search the commissioner's office and confiscate his computers. But the only evidence I had was a conversation with a deceased witness. I had nothing tangible to back up my allegations.

"I want you to find out everything you can about that bastard," Daniels said, pacing about the conference room. "Sit on him. If he so much as farts, I want to know about it. I want you two to nail his ass to the wall."

Daniels was pretty lit up about it. We all were.

I asked Denise to see what she could dig up on the commissioner. "I want a list of every development deal he's voted on. Let's see where the kickbacks are coming from."

"You got it."

"In the meantime, I say we have another chat with Heather Ingle. See if she knows anything."

I pulled my phone from my pocket and dialed her number. It went to voicemail. I left a message asking her to return my call as soon as possible. "It's urgent."

I tried calling her from JD's phone. She didn't have his number, and I figured she might have been avoiding my calls.

This time she picked up.

"Hello?"

"Heather," I said with a smile in my voice. "This is Deputy Wild."

"Who?"

She knew damn good and well *who*. "I have a few more questions for you about Crosby."

She hesitated a moment. "My lawyer has advised me not to speak with you."

"You're not a suspect. I just need to find out if Crosby ever talked to you about his job with the commissioner."

"My lawyer says never talk to cops."

"It sounds like you've got a good lawyer. But you don't need one. I promise you're not a suspect. Did Crosby ever mention the commissioner taking bribes in exchange for votes?"

"Not that I recall."

"We believe Crosby may have been extorting money from the commissioner to keep quiet. Do you recall if he suddenly came into a windfall?"

"I don't think he made a ton of money at that job. The only reason he took it was because he had political aspirations and thought it would be a good experience."

"I'm sure he would have made a fine politician." He had all the makings.

Heather sighed. "To tell you the truth, I usually paid when we went out. Crosby didn't come from money. And he never had a lot of it. But I guess over the last couple months, he did seem to have more cash. He started paying for more things." She paused. "Did you talk to that girl he worked with in the office? Megan, I think is her name."

"McKenzie."

"Yes, that's her. I think he had a thing for her. I don't know if they ever hooked up, and I don't want to know."

"I spoke with her. If it makes you feel better, she said Crosby wasn't her type." I paused. "She's dead, by the way."

Heather gasped. "What!?"

"She was involved in an *accident*," I said.

"And you think the commissioner may be involved?"

"That's where I'd put my money."

"I never liked that guy. I only met him a few times, but I got pervy vibes from him."

"If you can think of anything that might be helpful, please call."

She stammered, "I will."

I ended the call and dialed Isabella. "If I ask nicely, would you do another favor for me?"

"When have I not helped you out?"

I smiled.

I need you to look into Commissioner Johnson. He's taking bribes. I think one of the staff found out about it and put the screws on him. The guy is dirty, and I need to know where to look. Speaking of where to look, can you tell me where he is right now?"

Her fingers tapped the keys, and with a few strokes, she pulled his cellular information. "The phone that's listed in his name is currently at Forbidden Fruit. Tax dollars, hard at work."

"Hmm," I grunted, amused. "He was just talking about shutting the place down."

"I'll see what I can dig up on him. This should be fun. I like taking down corrupt officials."

"So do I, and there's no shortage of them."

A smile brightened JD's face when I informed him of our next destination.

"Was that your *source*?" Daniels asked.

I nodded.

He raised his hands innocently. "I don't want to know. But I'm glad you have resources."

## 33

C oconut Key was pure paradise—white sand beaches, teal water, perfect weather year-round, and beautiful sunsets. There were plenty of sights to see, but some of our favorite views were at *Forbidden Fruit.*

Toned bodies pranced the stage in stiletto heels. Spotlights slashed the hazy air. Pop music thumped through massive speakers. Exotic beauties writhed and undulated in hypnotic ways. Fleshy mounds bounced and jiggled. Green bills filled skimpy strings. Skin glistened with oil, and hearts were broken with each new dancer that took the stage.

Jacko leaned against the bar, overseeing his domain. He spotted us right away as we stepped into the dim club. He grinned and waved us over.

We greeted him with a smile and a handshake.

"I almost hate to ask," he said.

"Business," I replied.

"You can still have a round on the house," he said with a grin. "What brings you in today?"

"Commissioner Johnson," I said. "Have you seen him?"

"Yeah, he's right over there," he said, scanning the floor, then pointing.

"Don't be obvious about it."

He dropped his finger right away. Jacko leaned in and muttered, "What did he do?"

"A little of this, a little of that."

"Not at liberty to say. I got it."

The commissioner was too preoccupied to notice us. A luscious blonde was in his lap, grinding her cheeks against his crotch in a way that I'm sure could sway his vote.

"Who's the girl?" I asked.

"Misty."

She gave the commissioner a guided tour of her mountains.

The commissioner might talk a good game, but he would never actually push to shut this place down. Nobody would. It was everyone's guilty pleasure, and it was a cash cow for the fire marshal and other city inspectors. I didn't want to know how many palms Jacko had to grease to stay in business.

"Is the commissioner in here a lot?" I asked.

"Define *a lot*?"

"Once a week?"

"Maybe twice a week."

"Does he have a regular girl?"

"He seems to like a variety."

"Is his interest just limited to lap dances?"

Jacko raised his hands innocently, knowing what I was getting at. "Hey, I run a legitimate establishment here. You know that. But what happens in the Champagne Room is between the customer and the girl."

"Right."

"Love blossoms where it wants." He smiled. "You guys pretty much only work homicides. I'm guessing you have more than a casual interest in him."

"You're a smart man, Jacko. You're a smart man."

"Why don't you guys have a seat over there. That's rather inconspicuous," he said, pointing to a dim area of the club. "I'll send a round over and a couple girls to provide cover so you won't look so conspicuous."

"Much appreciated," JD said.

Jacko said, "Just remember my hospitality the next time Jacko gets himself in a bind."

I walked to the table and took a seat while JD hung back and exchanged a few words with Jacko.

After a moment, Jacko smiled and patted JD on the back as he walked away. Jack pulled out his phone and texted someone as he approached the table. He took a seat with a sly grin.

"What was that all about?"

"What was *what* all about?" Jack said innocently.

I knew better than to press further.

We watched the commissioner grope the young beauty in his lap.

Soon, a waitress was at our table, delivering two glasses of top-shelf whiskey. "Compliments of the house. Enjoy, gentlemen."

We lifted our glasses to toast and sipped the fine whiskey. It was smooth and heated my belly. Not a bad selection.

It wasn't long after that when two gorgeous entertainers approached—a blonde and a brunette.

"Howdy, gentlemen," the blonde said with a slight southern drawl. "Jacko says to show you a good time. You must be important."

The blonde plopped in JD's lap and the brunette in mine.

The raven-haired beauty's name was Lyric. Her green eyes, full lips, sculpted cheekbones, and luscious form were the perfect melody. Her matching black-lace bra and panties accentuated her delights. A black-lace garter belt and thigh-high stockings completed the ensemble.

"Want a dance?"

It was music to my ears.

Lyric stood up when the next song started and began to peel away the frilly articles. Her manicured fingers unclasped her bra, and the straps fell from her smooth shoulders. Her buoyant orbs bounced free.

My gaze was transfixed.

Soon, I had an up-close and personal view of her tantalizing peaks and valleys. Her warm body slithered against mine. Her wet lips whispered in my ear. Her breathy voice was like velvet, innocent and sinful. "Am I doing it right? This is my first time."

I almost died. "Trust me, you're a natural."

I didn't know if she was giving me a line or not. Either way, it was enjoyable and distracting. But I wasn't here for the distraction.

"Jacko says you're undercover and that we're helping you catch bad guys."

"Something like that."

"Does that mean you're going to deputize me?" she asked in a naughty voice. Her steamy breath hit my ear and sparked lustful thoughts. "I like handcuffs."

"I could be persuaded to arrest you."

"Only if you promise not to charge me."

"I bet you're definitely on the Most Wanted list."

She giggled and straddled my hips. Her delightful black panties rubbed against my shorts, and it would have been easy to forget all about the commissioner. The *captain* was ready to abandon the mission and start a new crusade.

The girls were allowed to touch you. You couldn't touch them unless invited. Even then, it was against the city ordinance.

Lyric continued to work her magic until the end of the song. It sure as hell didn't seem like her first time to me. She was a seasoned pro. I was sure of it.

The dance was over, and she fell back into my lap for casual conversation.

I looked across the club at the commissioner. Misty had done her job well. He had an equally delighted look on his face. Dario had been in the club for a while and put back a few drinks. It showed in his eyes.

A waitress delivered another round to his table, and she whispered something in Misty's ear.

A moment later, Misty stood up, took the commissioner by the hand, and led him through the tables toward the Champagne Room.

JD had a sly grin on his face. "Looks like the show is about to begin."

I knew he had cooked up some scheme with Jacko, and it was about to unfold.

## 34

"I texted your reporter friend," Jack said. "I told her to show up with a camera crew if she wanted a story."

Paris Delaney stepped into the club a moment later and looked around.

"Speak of the devil," JD said.

"If you'll excuse me," I said to Lyric. "Duty calls."

She made an adorable pouty face. "But I was starting to like being undercover with you."

"I'm sure there will be other missions." I dug into my pocket and handed her my card and a tip. "Thanks for the dance."

She smiled. "Any time."

JD waved Paris over. She approached the table as the girls left, and they exchanged glares. They didn't like the reporter interrupting their fun.

"I see you boys are working hard," Paris snarked.

"Where's your camera crew?" JD asked.

"Outside. Management doesn't take too kindly to video recording inside the establishment."

"You have a cell phone, don't you?" JD said.

"I do."

"So follow along and enjoy the show."

Jack climbed from his chair and marched toward the Champagne Room.

Paris followed and muttered in my ear, "What's he got up his sleeve?"

I shrugged.

She pulled her cell phone from her purse and readied the camera.

Jacko greeted us at the entrance to the Champagne Room. A bouncer stood guard. There was another lounge area with a stage, lights, tables, chairs, and comfy couches. The VIP lounge was exclusive and private.

Down a hallway were a row of actual champagne rooms.

Jacko's worried eyes flicked to Paris, then he muttered in JD's ear. "You never said she was going to be here. I'm going to draw a lot of heat on this one."

"Trust me. You're not going to be the one drawing the heat," JD said. "Where's he at?"

"In the Crystal Palace. "

Each room had its own unique name.

We pushed down the dim hallway. Sounds of pleasure emanated from the various rooms. It didn't take a brain surgeon to figure out what was going on inside.

You could get a little more handsy in the Champagne Room. Depending on how much you tipped, you could get *a lot* handsy. Maybe the girls would even get handsy with you. And sometimes, with the right girl, if you had deep enough pockets, you could go all the way.

We held up outside the door to the Crystal Palace. Jack nodded to Paris, who readied her camera phone. She hit *record* and Jack flung the door open. We burst into the room flashing our badges as the camera rolled.

The commissioner's eyes rounded, his nose dusted with powder. He'd been snorting fat lines off Misty's mountains.

Her peaks were snow-covered.

He sprang away from her, grabbed his trousers, and attempted to cover himself. "What's the meaning of this!"

"You're under arrest for possession of narcotics, soliciting prostitution... Shall I go on?" JD said.

The room was dim. The walls were red, and there was a small stage with a chrome pole and mirrors. There was a cozy loveseat against the wall and a queen bed with a vinyl mattress for easy cleanup.

This place went through wet wipes like nobody's business.

The commissioner looked straight into the camera, realizing just how screwed he was. He wiped the remnants of cocaine from his nose and tried to shield his face from the view of the camera, but it was too late.

JD pulled handcuffs from his pocket and jingled them. "Turn around and put your hands behind your head."

The commissioner's face reddened. "Let me get dressed first."

Nobody wanted to see the commissioner's flabby pale backside. We let him have his dignity.

He slid on his trousers and put on his shirt.

His unflattering naked form was a sight that couldn't be unseen. It was about to be broadcast across the island. Whatever the outcome, I was sure his political career was over. But then again, officials of other cities had been busted with crack cocaine and been re-elected. So, go figure.

JD ratcheted the cuffs around Dario's wrists, and the commissioner made blustery threats. "You're making a big mistake. Do you know who I am?"

"Indeed we do, Commissioner," JD said.

I pulled on a pair of nitrile gloves and confiscated the little brown vial of cocaine that sat on an end table by the bed.

Paris had an ear-to-ear grin on her face as she soaked up the scandalous footage of the commissioner.

JD escorted him out of the room, and Jacko directed us toward a rear exit down the hallway so his arrest wouldn't spook the other patrons.

Misty licked her finger in a lewd manner, then used the wet digit to mop up the cocaine residue on her buxom breasts. She rubbed the powder against her gums for a little boost. "I'm not going to get in any trouble, am I?"

There wasn't a hint of concern in her voice.

"Jacko assured me I was doing you a favor."

"Whose cocaine was it?" I asked.

"Not mine," she said slyly.

"And did the commissioner proposition you for sex?"

"Indeed, he did."

"And you're willing to testify?"

She smiled. "Yes, I am."

"Then I'm sure you won't get in trouble."

"Who's going to reimburse me for expenses?" She glanced at the half-empty vial of cocaine in my gloved hand and the copious amounts that spilled onto the floor.

Jacko appeared in the doorway. He dug into his pocket and peeled off several crisp hundred dollar bills and handed them to Misty. "This ought to cover any damages."

She took the money with a smile and stuffed it into her bra. "Thank you, kind sir." Her sultry eyes flicked to me. "Am I free to go?"

"You need to make an official statement," I said.

I got her real name and contact info and recorded her statement on my phone.

After she left, Jacko said, "You know you owe me big time."

"I know."

Jacko was a nice guy, but the cash didn't come from the goodness of his heart. I was sure JD had made prior arrangements with him that I was unaware of. And, as far as I was concerned, I would stay unaware of those arrangements.

I thanked Jacko, then exited through the rear door. The blinding sun squinted my eyes.

JD hung onto the commissioner, waiting for a patrol car to arrive.

Paris continued to film on her cell phone, asking the commissioner questions.

"You recently called for a ban on adult establishments in Coconut Key," Paris said. "Has your position changed?"

He glared at her.

"What about your anti-drug, non-profit organization? Does this compromise its integrity?"

The commissioner looked like he was about to explode. His face reddened, and the veins in his neck pulsed. Sweat misted on his skin. For him, the patrol car couldn't get here fast enough. He looked like he'd do just about anything to get away from Paris Delaney.

Mendoza pulled into the parking lot a few moments later, and JD stuffed the commissioner into the back of the patrol car.

Mendoza grinned with amusement.

Once the commissioner was secure, JD tapped on the quarter panel, and Mendoza drove away.

Paris turned the camera on me and asked, "Deputy Wild, can you give us details of this sting operation?"

I reached my hand out and grasped the phone from her pretty fingers. I stopped the recording, then handed the phone back to her. "Just be thankful for the scoop."

She grinned. "Scoops are always appreciated. You two never cease to amuse me."

"We keep you in business," JD said. "That's what we do."

We'd certainly given her more than her fair share of headlines.

JD and I made our way back to the Porsche and headed toward the station to fill out after-action reports.

"I don't want to know," I said to JD along the way.

"What's there to know?"

"How this all went down."

"We saw the commissioner on his lunch break. He repeatedly violated city ordinance, touching a dancer inappropriately. We saw him enter a Champagne Room with the dancer. The two had been acting suspicious, and we had reason to believe a crime was in progress when we entered the Crystal Palace."

It was all true. But the bust was questionable at best. I wasn't sure the whole thing would hold up. But I had no doubt that Commissioner Johnson would be tendering his resignation shortly.

At the station, we let him sit in the interrogation room for a while before grilling him.

## 35

The overhead fluorescents flickered and buzzed. Commissioner Johnson sweated. The pits of his shirt were soaked. He glared at us as we entered the room and took a seat across the table from him. "This was entrapment. She lured me into that room to talk."

"To *talk*," I mirrored incredulously.

"Then she disrobed and began engaging in drug use."

"Drugs which you accidentally happened to inhale."

"She grabbed my head and forced it against her bosoms. Any residue on my body was a result of that transfer."

"*Forced*," I snarked again.

He was still wired.

"And just how did your clothes get on the floor?" I asked just to see what kind of answer he could come up with.

"I spilled a drink on my trousers. I merely removed them to dry them out."

I chuckled. "That's a good one. I'm sure your constituency will believe that. After all, you do have the *most popular poll numbers of any sitting commissioner.*"

His eyes narrowed at me. "Entrapment. A setup."

"I'm sure you're aware, Commissioner, that entrapment only applies to government officials. A private citizen cannot entrap another citizen."

"The cocaine wasn't mine. It was that harlot's. I was merely trying to listen to her troubles and offer helpful advice. These girls have all kinds of issues, and I try to lead them to the Lord."

I almost choked on that one. "So, you visit the establishment on a regular basis doing missionary work?"

"If I can save one wayward soul." He made his best attempt at sincerity.

"The wayward soul that you need to save is your own, Commissioner. The drug and solicitation charges are the least of your worries."

His face crinkled with confusion.

"I'd be more concerned with the bribery and corruption charges."

"Excuse me?"

"And conspiracy to commit murder. That's the big one."

He balked. "I don't know what you're talking about."

"We know you were taking bribes in exchange for development deals. We know that Crosby found out, and he was extorting money from you. You had him eliminated."

"That's preposterous."

"I agree. It's pretty outrageous. But it's the truth."

"You can't prove that."

"McKenzie Malloy was on to you as well. Didn't you find it odd that she suffered a fatal car accident?"

He hung his head and attempted a solemn tone. "Another terrible tragedy. But that has nothing to do with me."

"You know what I think. I think you got into bed with some really bad people. I think they're cleaning up loose ends. I'd be careful, Commissioner. You might find yourself cleaned as well."

His eyes rounded, and he swallowed hard.

"If I were you, I'd start talking now. Otherwise, you're going to be looking at a really long stretch that I don't think you are suited for."

Dario said nothing, but I could tell my words were bouncing around in his head. "I'd like to speak with an attorney."

"An attorney can't help you. Your career is over. And I'm determined to put you away."

Jack leaned in and whispered. "Pro tip." He pointed at me. "You do not want that guy gunning for you."

The chair screeched as Jack pushed away from the table. I followed him to the door and knocked. A guard buzzed us out.

Dario was in for a rude awakening. I'm sure he would find his first night in a holding cell most enjoyable.

Daniels joined us in the hallway, having watched from the observation room. "Tell me you've got something more on this clown."

"I do," Denise said with a smile as she approached.

We all waited eagerly.

"Dario has voted on several development deals. I found one for a low-income housing project with a forgivable loan. The property was never built."

"Who was the contractor?"

"Maverick Foxwell. His company has been the recipient of multiple deals. None of which have ever been completed." She paused. "You know, there may be more than one commissioner involved in this."

I grimaced. "How's the money coming back to Dario?"

"I don't know yet."

"Super PAC," JD said. "They're not bound by contribution limits. They just can't give the money directly to the politician. Money goes to the developer. They kick a portion back to the PAC via some offshore company or some other donor. The PAC spends the money on consulting or some nebulous crap. And that funnels into the commissioner's pocket."

"I'll keep digging," Denise said.

"There's a money trail somewhere. Find it."

"I'm all over it."

The interview with Dario was over. He'd asked for an attorney, and we had to stop questioning him. But I poked my head back into the interrogation room and said two words.

## 36

D ario swallowed hard when I said, "Maverick Foxwell."

I left him to chew on that for a while.

"I think someone is trying to kill me," Paris said when she called.

"Who did you piss off now?" I asked.

"The Candy Killer."

"Is that what you're calling him?"

"It's the best I could do."

"And why do you think the Candy Killer is trying to kill you?"

She huffed. "I need you to take this seriously."

"I am taking this seriously."

"Somebody left a box of chocolates and a dozen blue roses on my doorstep."

"Who is it from?"

"The card says from a secret admirer."

"What's the matter? You don't think you have any real admirers?"

"Tyson!"

"Sorry."

"I have plenty of real admirers, I'll have you know."

"What makes you think it's from the killer?"

"Well, for starters, have you tried to buy a box of chocolates recently? Didn't think so. There aren't any Valentine's Day chocolates available on the entire island. It's all been pulled from the shelves. Plus, I made some pretty insulting comments about him on air."

"I saw that. Newsflash. Maybe you shouldn't insult homicidal maniacs."

"You do that all the time."

"I'm a trained professional."

She scoffed.

"I saved your ass, didn't I?"

"And I am forever in your debt."

"Don't touch anything. I'm on my way over."

I caught JD up to speed, and we headed to Paris's new condo. She recently moved into the Trident Tower. It was a luxury high rise with stunning views, an attached marina, and all the desirable amenities. It was home to socialites, tech types, investment bankers, celebrities, and a few gangsters. Now it was home to the island's most ambitious reporter.

JD pulled under the carport, and the valet rushed to get his door. Jack slapped a $20 in his hand and told him to keep the car up front.

We stepped to the glass door, and the pretty blonde concierge buzzed us in.

"Who are you here for today?" she asked as we strolled inside.

"Paris Delaney," I said.

Her eyes rounded with concern. "She hasn't done anything wrong, has she?"

I chuckled. "No. Have you been working all day?"

"Since 9 AM."

"Do you recall a floral delivery for Ms. Delaney?"

"Yeah. A guy on a motorcycle. I buzzed him in, and he went right up. He had a dozen beautiful roses and a box of chocolates." She gasped. "Oh, no! Chocolate. You don't think...?"

"We're not sure. Did you get a good look at him?"

"No. He pulled up on his bike, took the flowers and candies from a compartment on the back, and strolled in. He was still wearing his helmet. I didn't think anything about it. A lot of the delivery guys are in and out so quickly they leave their helmets on. Sometimes their visor is up, sometimes it's not."

"You get a license plate?"

She frowned. "No. Sorry."

"What about security cameras?"

"No cameras. Residents vetoed that idea."

"What did the bike look like?"

"Two wheels, a seat, and a tank."

"That's helpful."

"Sorry. I don't know much about bikes."

"Was it sporty or was it a cruiser?"

"Definitely sporty. Looked like a racing bike."

"Thanks."

"Sorry, I couldn't be more help. Is Ms. Delaney okay?"

"As far as I know. She hasn't eaten the candy."

A relieved breath escaped her lungs. "That would be so tragic if our new resident died. I like her. I think she's spunky. I know everybody loves to hate her, but she's been really nice to me."

We strolled across the opulent lobby to the elevators. I pressed the call button, and a moment later, the bell rang, and the doors slid open.

We stepped aboard, and I pressed the button for floor 24. We rocketed upwards, got off the lift, and ambled down the hallway.

Paris waited for us by her door. She looked relieved to see us. "See, someone is trying to kill me," she said, pointing to the offending items.

"Have you touched anything?"

She shook her head.

I snapped on a pair of nitrile gloves and picked up the box of chocolate. It was still sealed with shrink-wrap, but it didn't look mass-produced. It looked like someone had purchased shrink-wrap material and used a heat gun to seal it. It would pass inspection at a quick glance, but serious scrutiny would reveal the flaws.

"I think the flowers are safe, but we'll take this back to the lab and have it analyzed. It looks suspicious."

"How do I know the flowers aren't poisoned as well? Perhaps some chemical has been sprayed on them that causes death when inhaled."

"That might be a tad dramatic."

Her eyes narrowed at me.

"Okay. We'll have the lab look at the flowers too."

"You sure know how to antagonize people," JD said.

"Me? I do no such thing. I report the news. Sometimes it's not what people want to hear, but the truth can be ugly."

I rolled my eyes. "It seems like you've struck a nerve with the Candy Killer. I think maybe you should keep it up."

She looked at me like I was crazy. "You want me to antagonize a man that's trying to kill me?"

"Maybe we can draw him out."

She thought about it for a moment, her eyes staring into mine. "What do you want me to do?"

## 37

"I'd like to open tonight's segment with a plea to the Candy Killer," Paris said, standing under the lights in the television studio.

The green screen behind her was replaced digitally in real time with the newsroom background. A large broadcast camera focused on her.

We watched a monitor from the side of the stage. Breaking news graphics appeared on the screen. *Special Report.*

Paris continued. "I recently received flowers and chocolate which law enforcement officers suspect may have been tainted by the Candy Killer."

It would take days for the lab results to come back, even with expedited priority.

"I believe this attack is in response to my previous segment. What's the matter? Are you too thin-skinned to take criticism? I welcome you to call into the show and explain your actions. I stand by my former statement. Targeting faceless, nameless victims is an act of cowardice. Targeting me directly, while a departure from the random nature of your crimes, is a weak and pathetic attempt at relevance." Paris made a pouty face, mocking the killer. "Did you get dumped? Hurt by someone you love? Are you lashing out in anger, unable to control your emotions? Grow up. We all suffer pain. We all suffer loss. It's how we handle the challenges that life presents that define us as human beings. It displays our character. And you, sir, have no character."

A phone number was displayed on the screen.

"There's the number to the station. Feel free to call and discuss this at any time. Let our audience know your true motivations."

The instant the number was displayed, the phone lines lit up. Station operators screened the calls while Paris continued her segment.

I didn't have much confidence the killer would actually call the station. He would have to be a fool to make a phone call from a traceable number.

"Now for a shocking revelation about corruption in Coconut Key. Earlier today, Commissioner Dario Johnson was arrested at a local adult establishment and charged with soliciting prostitution and possession of cocaine."

The footage Paris captured on her cell phone displayed on the screen. Pixelated squares obscured views of private parts and saved the audience from a ghastly sight.

"The commissioner has been implicated in numerous crimes, including the fraudulent allocation of taxpayer funds. We investigated the commissioner's sketchy connection to a local developer, Maverick Foxwell, whose company was the recipient of multiple forgivable loans." She went on to describe the scheme in detail. "We caught up with Maverick at his luxury estate in Stingray Bay, but he declined to comment when we brought up the alleged fraud."

The segment cut to clips of the sprawling estate. There was a silver Land Rover in the driveway along with a white Lamborghini Huracán. Paris knocked on Maxwell's door. There was a brief exchange through the video doorbell.

"Can you tell me why none of the projects have been started? Where is the money? How much did you kick back to Commissioner Johnson?"

The segment cut to a close-up of the video doorbell. It crackled as Maverick disconnected.

Paris continued from the studio, "We asked Maverick about the death of Crosby Gallagher, the commissioner's chief of staff—a victim of the tragic slaying at the Frisky Kitty. We also asked about the hit-and-run death of McKenzie Malloy, who replaced Crosby as the top aid in Commissioner Johnson's office. She had recently contacted law enforcement about the alleged corruption."

The segment cut to a clip of Maverick peering through the blinds, glaring at the camera crew.

"As of tonight's broadcast, Commissioner Johnson is in custody, awaiting arraignment. No charges have been brought for his alleged corruption and possible involvement in the deaths of his staff. We will continue to monitor the situation and bring you up-to-the-minute information."

It was a scathing exposé on the commissioner.

The camera cut, and Paris greeted us off stage. A devious smirk curled her plump lips. "How's that for antagonistic?"

"You have a gift," I said. "I'll give you that."

A frazzled PA approached. "We've received dozens of calls, and they're still coming in. We're trying to sort through them. A lot of guys claiming to be the killer, but none of them knew the correct type of flowers that were sent to you. So far, it's a lot of guys just making lewd comments."

"I'll need the numbers of everyone who calls in," I said.

The PA nodded.

Paris's cell phone rang from an unknown number. She looked at the display with hesitation before answering.

"Hello?"

She listened intently, then mouthed the words, "I think it's him."

She put the call on speaker.

"How did you get this number?" Paris asked.

"The same way I got your home address," the man said.

"Well, the flowers were pretty. What kind were they?"

"Blue roses."

"Any particular meaning?"

"Mystery, desire, unattainable love."

"So, you're in love with me?"

He laughed. "I think you're in love with yourself."

I stifled a chuckle.

Paris glared at me, then addressed the Candy Killer. "That's not a very nice thing to say."

"It's the ugly truth."

"Why are you doing this?"

"Because I feel like it."

"Who hurt you?"

"That's none of your business."

"Is that what this is all about? Your broken heart?"

I texted Isabella and asked her to track Paris's phone.

"Are you hoping that your ex will randomly pick up one of these boxes of chocolate?" Paris asked.

"The odds of that would be slim. But I wouldn't cry if that happened."

"You sound like a caring, compassionate individual," she snarked. "It's no wonder your ex left you."

"My ex was a narcissistic abuser. I hope she gets hit by a bus and chokes on her own blood."

Paris made a disgusted face. "It sounds like you have a lot of anger inside."

"Gee, how did you ever figure that out?"

"And you think that poisoning random strangers is somehow going to be a cathartic experience?"

He said nothing.

"Two people have already died. Has that diminished your rage? Are you any less angry? Do you feel better?"

She waited for a response, but he didn't speak.

"Those people had friends and families. People that cared about them. Those people are now in pain, mourning the loss. Doesn't that bother you?"

"Life's a bitch."

"How many people have to die before you move on?"

"Maybe I'll never move on."

"How many more items are out there that you've poisoned?"

"I don't know. Most everything has been pulled off the shelves. Perhaps I'll need to find a new treat to taint. But then you might have to change my name. If I stopped poisoning candy, what would you call me?"

"A sadistic jackass."

He laughed. "Maybe I should focus all of my attention on you. You sort of remind me of my ex."

"If you promise to stop poisoning random products, then by all means, target me."

"How noble," he snarked.

"Who is your ex?"

"Do you think I'm stupid?"

"I think you lack the skills necessary to self evaluate."

"I'm fully aware of my flaws," he said.

"Is your ex alive or dead?"

"I haven't killed her yet."

I listened intently for any sound that might give away his location.

Isabella texted a moment later. He's calling from a payphone at the Highland Village Mall.

I mouthed the words to Paris, "Keep him on the line."

JD and I rushed out of the studio and hopped into the Porsche. We sped across the island, racing toward the mall. I knew exactly where he was calling from. There was a bank of pay phones near the restrooms by the service center. It was one of the few pay phones left on the island. You could find them here and there, but who needed a pay phone when everyone had a mobile device in their pocket?

## 38

J D valet parked at the mall. We sprinted through the open-air courtyard. I had called the sheriff along the way and told him to send the forensic team.

The smell of pizza and hamburgers wafted from the food court. Leggy beauties pranced around in stiletto heels with designer handbags dangling from manicured fingers. Highland Village was full of designer boutiques with bespoke clothing, jewelry, and handbags. Retail therapy for Coconut Key's elite.

We weaved through pedestrians, running past benches and potted trees. We turned a few corners and sprinted down the long hall to the public restrooms, across from the administrative offices and security.

There was a single pay phone on the wall.

At one point in time, there had been dozens. The outline remained on the wall where they had been removed.

The Candy Killer was long gone.

We stood guard at the phone, waiting for the forensic team to arrive. I wanted them to dust for prints, though I was sure our killer was smarter than that.

I called Paris. She answered right away.

"How long were you able to keep him on the phone?"

"We hung up maybe a minute ago. We chatted for a good while. That dude has a screw loose. Maybe a few."

My face tensed. "We just missed him."

I nodded to JD, and he ran back down the hallway to scan the courtyard, looking for anyone who resembled the perp. He disappeared around the corner a moment later.

A cute girl entered the hall and made her way toward me. Her high heels clattered in the narrow passage. The pink designer dress fell to her mid thighs. A white Birkin bag hung from her forearm. As she drew near, she reached to use the phone.

I blocked her. "Sorry. Phone's off-limits."

Her face crinkled. "Says who?"

I pulled my badge from my pocket.

Her face twisted into a frown. "Well, can I use your phone? It's an emergency."

I told Paris I'd call her back. "You're not making a call halfway around the world, are you?"

"No."

"You're not purchasing drugs, are you?"

She huffed. "My battery's dead. Okay?"

I handed her the phone, and she dialed a number. She started chatting with a friend.

A guy emerged from the restroom and passed by. He looked the girl up and down, and I didn't blame him. She was cute. A little snotty but cute.

Then his eyes flicked to me, then to the phone, then back to me as he continued to pass.

As he walked down the hallway, a flash flickered in my mind —the security footage from Coconut Grocery. I recognized the design on the back of his shirt—a sportbike racing around the track. It was the same garment worn by the Candy Killer during his first return.

"Freeze! Coconut County."

The dude burst into a sprint, and I chased after him. My sneakers slapped against the tile, echoing in the hallway.

He rounded the corner and darted into the courtyard.

I raced out of the hallway and caught sight of him. I glanced over my shoulder at JD. He was talking to two cute girls, oblivious to me.

I shouted at Jack and continued after the Candy Killer.

He weaved through the mall patrons, bumping shoulders with oncoming traffic, disrupting shopping bags.

He smacked into a woman exiting a store.

She tumbled to the ground, and something glass inside her bag shattered.

The woman shrieked, her knees skinned from the fall.

I continued after the perp, my heart thumping, my chest heaving.

Candy Killer rounded another corner.

Patrons gasped and gawked.

I cautiously followed.

A mall security guard walked in the opposite direction.

I shouted, "Coconut County. Stop that man!"

The security guard focused on the Candy Killer. He made a half-assed attempt to block his path, but the guard wasn't exactly in the best shape of his life, and he couldn't get across the courtyard in time.

The perp rounded another corner and sprinted into the parking lot.

I was gaining on him.

He looked back over his shoulder at me as he ran.

Cars cruised about, looking for parking spaces.

The perp darted in front of one and slipped down an aisle.

I was getting closer.

Candy Killer gave a nervous glance over his shoulder again just as a car backed out of a space. He smacked into the rear quarter panel, twisted around, and kept going—this time with a little limp.

I was right on top of him.

I didn't feel like tackling him to the ground and eating the pavement. When I got close, I just kicked his foot, tripping him.

He face planted against the tarmac, getting a good amount of road rash on his palms and face.

I pounced on him. He tried to buck me off, but I grabbed the back of his hair and smashed his head against the tarmac a couple times.

"Okay, okay!" he cried.

I ratcheted the cuffs around his wrists, then yanked the scumbag to his feet. I read him his rights, called for a patrol unit, and dragged him back toward the mall.

JD caught up with me about the time Mendoza arrived.

"Thanks for the assist," I said, my voice thick with sarcasm.

"I was preoccupied. Did you see that brunette? She's right up your alley." He smiled and said in singsong, "I got phone numbers."

I stuffed the Candy Killer into the back of the patrol car, and Mendoza ran his information.

According to his driver's license, his name was Owen Lloyd. Mendoza looked up his DMV records. Sure enough, a red Yamazuki CVX 600 was registered in his name.

I asked Owen, "Where's your bike parked?"

"I'm not telling you shit."

"Don't worry. I'll find it."

Mendoza drove the perp to the station, and we searched the parking lot.

We found the red sportbike. Attached to it was a helmet that looked exactly like the one in the security video. The same red demon printed atop the crown.

A slight grin tugged my lips.

I took the helmet and gloves and called the department to have the bike impounded as evidence.

I borrowed Jack's phone and called my cell. After a few rings, the girl who borrowed it answered. "Hello?"

"I need to get my phone back."

"Okay. You just took off. So, I didn't know what to do."

I asked her to meet us at the valet stand, and she showed up a few minutes later and handed the phone back to me.

"Thanks again," she said.

JD drank in her form as she spun around and sauntered back to the mall. "She could borrow my phone anytime."

The valet pulled the Porsche around, and we hopped in and zipped back to the station.

Candy Killer was processed and printed. We let him sit in the interrogation room and work up a sweat before entering. JD and I took our usual seats across the table from the perp.

I set the helmet on the table.

"I ain't saying shit to you."

"That's fine. Makes no difference. The forensic team will find your fingerprints on the pay phone."

"What does that prove?"

## 39

"It proves you used the phone," I said, knowing it didn't.

"It proves I touched the phone," he said.

At least he admitted touching the phone.

"You called Paris Delaney. You admitted poisoning and killing two people."

"I didn't admit to anything. I didn't call anyone. I don't know what you're talking about."

"We found your motorcycle in the parking lot."

"So. I had to get to the mall somehow."

"This your helmet?"

"Looks like mine."

"I've got video footage of you returning chocolates wearing that helmet. I've got an eyewitness at the Trident Tower that will testify you delivered the flowers and chocolates to Paris Delaney wearing that same helmet."

He scoffed. "Nothing with nothing sauce. So somebody wore the same brand of helmet as me. Dime a dozen. Doesn't prove anything."

"Paris can identify your voice."

"Over the phone? No way that holds up. I'm not your guy. Try harder."

This guy was starting to piss me off.

"Guess what, smart guy. We got a warrant. Deputies are searching your place. Something tells me we're going to find strychnine, syringes, shrink-wrap, and probably several boxes of candy. When you put all that circumstantial evidence together, it's gonna be enough for you to go down. Two counts of murder. You're looking at life." I paused for dramatic effect. "Is that still nothing with nothing sauce?"

He swallowed hard.

We stared at each other for a long moment.

Daniels pushed into the interrogation room. He whispered something in my ear, and I smiled.

He stood back, leaned against the wall, and folded his arms.

Owen's nervous eyes flicked between us.

"Looks like our deputies hit the jackpot. Do I need to tell you again what they found?"

We hadn't even searched his place yet.

Sweat misted on his forehead.

"Do us both a favor," I said. "Confess now, save us all the trouble, and maybe we can get you into a nice cushy facility where your ass won't turn into a glory hole."

The magnitude of the situation was beginning to weigh on him. "You don't know how many more items are out there that are poisoned."

"Now we're getting somewhere."

"You give me a reduced sentence. I'll make sure no one ever eats the poison."

"You better hurry up and tell us before someone else dies."

"1 or 20, what's the difference now?"

My eyes narrowed at him. It wasn't the first time that I'd heard that kind of rhetoric, and it always made me sick to my stomach. "I'm sure it makes a lot of difference to the friends and loved ones of the victims."

"Manslaughter, and I walk in 15."

I stifled a chuckle. "You acted with malice aforethought. These were premeditated. That's murder one."

"I never intended to kill anyone."

I lifted an incredulous eyebrow. "What did you think would happen when you poisoned candy with strychnine?"

He shrugged. "I thought maybe somebody might get an upset stomach."

It was bullshit, and we both knew it.

He clearly had some degree of familiarity with the law. "You acted with a clear disregard for human life. You're not going to walk with a slap on the wrist."

"I had no intention to kill anyone," he repeated. "Manslaughter, 15 years. Two counts to serve concurrently." He paused. "It's that or no deal. If somebody else dies, it's on your hands now."

I frowned and exchanged a glance with Sheriff Daniels.

---

## 40

We spoke with Daniels in the hallway.

"No way that punk walks in 15 for what he did. Hell, for all we know, there are no additional poisoned candies out there. It's all been pulled from the shelf, anyway."

"What if he moved on from candy?" I suggested. "What if other items are tainted?"

The sheriff frowned. "I'll talk to the state attorney."

Daniels made a phone call. JD and I listened intently as he discussed the situation. There was a little back and forth. He didn't look terribly thrilled when he hung up.

"Tell that punk if we recover more items that test positive for strychnine, and if nobody else dies, he can do his 15, plus 15 years probation. But he makes a full confession right now."

I didn't want to see the scumbag get off easy, but I didn't want anyone else to suffer a horrible fate either.

We pushed back into the interrogation room and made the offer. Owen took the deal and told us where we could find more poisoned items. I called the manager of Coconut Grocery and directed him to pull all of the chocolate chip ice creams.

Owen assured me that nothing else was compromised.

"You sure you're not accidentally forgetting anything?"

"No. I swear," he said. "That's everything."

"This deal goes bye-bye if anyone else dies, you understand?"

He nodded.

"Was it worth it?" I asked, staring him dead in the eyes.

He didn't really have an answer for that. He just shrugged. Owen would have a long time to think about it, that was for sure.

I wouldn't be eating any chocolate chip ice cream or Valentine's Day candy anytime soon, though.

We left the station and headed to Oyster Avenue. We grabbed something to eat at Gators and ended up at our usual haunt, *Tide Pool*.

We kicked back by the outdoor pool, sipping whiskey, watching scantily clad beauties frolic in the water. Strawberry daiquiris, mixed with the smell of chlorine, wafted through the air. Music pumped, and pretty people mixed and mingled.

We'd been there about an hour when I got the most unusual phone call. I didn't recognize the number.

"Tyson?" a woman asked.

"You got him."

"I don't know if you remember me. We met the other day on Tristan's yacht?"

I pretended not to remember. "Were you the blonde?"

She laughed. "How many girls did you meet on Tristan's yacht?"

"I met a really cute brunette. Can't remember her name, though." I remembered her name.

"I don't know if I should be hurt that you don't remember my name or excited that you thought I was cute."

"You know damn good and well you're cute."

"It's always nice to hear."

"I'm sure you hear it a lot."

"Well, aren't you full of compliments. Maybe I should call you more often."

"Maybe you should. I was beginning to think I would never hear from you."

"It's not that I didn't want to call you. I just got busy, and I hadn't anticipated staying in town this long."

"But you've had a sudden change of plans. You've realized that you can't live without me."

She chuckled. "Something like that. Actually, I have a problem that I'm hoping you can help me with."

I lifted an intrigued eyebrow. "So, this is a business call."

"It's a little of both. My problem is your problem, too."

I tensed slightly. "You're not pregnant, are you?"

She laughed again. "We didn't get that far, remember? I mean, you didn't hook up with another brunette, did you?"

"Not that I recall. What is this problem you speak of?"

"First, I think we should be totally honest with each other. Lies are no way to start a relationship."

"We're starting a relationship?"

"Yes, I've decided that we are."

I grinned, growing more and more intrigued. "You've decided?"

"Yes, I have."

"I'm listening."

"My name's not Kendall."

"Oh, really?"

"You know how it is. I meet a lot of strange people, sometimes I don't like to give out my name right away."

"Are you calling me strange?"

"Unique."

"Fair enough. What's your real name?"

"Do you believe in ESP?"

It was kind of out of left field, but I decided to play along. "I don't know. I have a friend who claims to be psychic. Sometimes she is, sometimes she isn't. Is it luck? Is it intuition? Is it something more? Hard to say."

"I'm going to describe our problem. After I'm done, I'm sure your intuition will let you guess my name."

"How big of a problem is this?"

"I think you'll agree it's pretty big. At first, I think you might be mad. But then you'll realize that we both have a mutual interest."

"Enough games."

"You lost a jewel, did you not?"

She had my full attention. "I did."

"We have a lot in common because so did I."

I put it all together. "Lily Lovelace."

"See, you may be psychic after all."

The name drew JD's attention. He leaned in, listening intently.

"You stole the Jewel of Aphrodite," I said. "And now you're telling me someone stole it from you?"

"You are good at your job," she said, mocking me.

"You're admitting to felony theft."

"I'm hoping you can overlook the felony theft part."

I laughed. "Why would I do that?"

"Because I can help you get the jewel back."

"And why would you do that?"

"Because I'm a vindictive bitch. And I don't want Charles Le Grand to get away with the stone."

"And what's in this for you?"

"The satisfaction of putting a wrench in Le Grand's plan. And of course immunity from prosecution."

"Of course," I snarked. "You know, I've heard a lot about you."

"Oooh, please tell me. I love to hear gossip about myself."

"They tell me you're not to be trusted."

"I'm being perfectly honest with you. There is honor among thieves. I always hold to my word. I've never screwed over a partner."

"I'm not so sure about that. What about all the men that you've duped?"

"Fools that were interested in me for one thing. They got what they deserved."

"You honestly expect me to work with you to recover the jewel?"

"What choice do you really have, Deputy? Do you have any leads? Do you know where Charles Le Grand is? Do you know where he is meeting the buyer?"

I said nothing.

"Didn't think so." She paused. "I'll give you 15 seconds to think about it. Then I hang up the phone, and you never see or hear from me again. Or, you take a leap of faith, and we both walk away happy."

## 41

"Where is Le Grand making the exchange?" I asked.

"You didn't answer my question. Do we have a deal?"

"Why don't you come down to the station, and we can talk about it?"

She laughed. "Is that a *no*?"

"I haven't decided yet."

"Time is running out."

"Tell me where the exchange is taking place?"

"No. You have a leak in your department. You can't bring anyone else in on this if you ever want to see that ruby again. Word will get out. The mission could be compromised."

"Where does your intel come from?"

"It's my job to assess threats and weaknesses. You think I'd walk into your town and pull a job without knowing anything about local law enforcement?"

"Perhaps you know more about our organization than I do. Who's the leaker?"

"Tick-tock, Deputy."

"What's your angle?"

"I told you. I want to see the look on Le Grand's face when we take the jewel away from him."

"What about Anatoly?"

"He hired two people to do the same job. I don't work that way."

"It's smart business. Redundant systems."

She didn't like that. "Time's up. Looks like I'm on my own."

"Wait. Not so fast."

"Does that mean we have a deal?"

"I'm willing to explore this."

"That's rather non-committal."

"Prove you're worth committing to. I mean, we really don't know each other."

"Perhaps we should spend more time together? Build trust."

"Trust is essential. We're having a drink at Tide Pool. You could always join us."

She paused for a long moment. "How do I know I'm not walking into a setup?"

"You'll just have to take a leap of faith."

"If I smell anything funny, I'm gone. And you'll never get the ruby."

She ended the call, and I exchanged a glance with JD. He'd heard most of the conversation, but I filled him in on the details.

"This should be interesting. Think she's full of shit?"

"I think that's a distinct possibility. But at this point, what do we have to lose?"

I saw no need to arrest Lily Lovelace when she showed up. I had nothing on her except for her admission, which she would deny. I had little to back it up. She didn't seem to be in possession of the jewel, but that could have been a lie as well. This could all be a cunning ruse to throw me off the trail, but I wasn't on the trail. She'd gotten away clean.

Heads turned as Lily sauntered into *Tide Pool*, looking like a million bucks. The short leather mini skirt and strappy heels accentuated her toned legs. A deep-V halter top inspired wanton thoughts. She strutted to the table and wiggled her fingers. "Evening, boys. Good to see you both."

I drank in her form. There was no doubt she had a talent for stealing hearts.

We stood up like gentlemen and offered her a seat. JD gave up his chair and pulled another close. She sat in between us.

"What are you drinking?" I asked.

"Whiskey. Rocks."

I flagged over a waitress. She took the diabolical vixen's drink order and sauntered away.

"I've taken the first step toward trust." Lily looked around for other officers or federal agents.

"And I'm taking steps by not arresting you."

She rolled her eyes. "You don't want to arrest me. I'm too much fun on the loose."

"When is Charles Le Grand meeting Anatoly?" I asked, getting down to business.

"I'm monitoring the situation."

"If you were monitoring the situation, how did you lose the gem in the first place?"

"Everyone makes mistakes. Miscalculations. I'd rather not get into it. See, Deputy, this is a matter of pride and reputation. Nobody steals from me."

I chuckled. "A thief that doesn't like being stolen from."

"Feels like more of a double-cross to me."

"Why do you need us?"

"Because it's not a job that can be done alone. It's always good to have a buddy, is it not?"

I looked at JD. "It's indispensable."

"And I know you won't screw me over," she said. "You've got quite the impressive resume. You're loyal to a fault. You're smart, capable, and dangerous. A good person to have on one's team."

"Flattery will get you everywhere," I said.

A mischievous smile tugged her full lips. "I know talent when I see it."

"How can you be so sure you know where the exchange will take place?"

"Because I put a tracker aboard Anatoly's vessel."

I lifted an impressed eyebrow. "So the exchange will be made at sea?"

She nodded.

"And how did you get this tracker aboard?"

"I have my ways."

I gave her a look that demanded a better explanation.

"I know this may come as a shock to you. But I'm going to let you in on a little secret. You boys tend to let your guard down when a beautiful woman pays even the slightest bit of attention to you. It's really quite incredible. You get a whiff of it, and you lose IQ points."

I couldn't argue. We've all done dumb things at times in the name of love or lust.

"So, you seduced Anatoly and planted a tracker on his yacht?"

She scoffed. "No, I didn't seduce that troll. I hired someone to do it. A gorgeous blonde. Name's Annabelle. Wavy hair down to her ass crack. Long legs. A body to die for. You'd like her. It wasn't hard to infiltrate the yacht. She planted the device. And I've been tracking it for weeks now."

"You always spy on your employers?"

"I like to be prepared. Information is power."

"And what if Anatoly finds your tracking device?"

"I still have my asset in the field."

"She's aboard his ship?"

"As we speak. It seems he took a liking to her."

"Where is Anatoly's ship now?"

She smiled. "You keep asking me that."

"You keep declining to answer."

## 42

---

"We need to act fast, gentlemen," Lily said. "My source tells me the exchange is going down tomorrow night."

"Why not have your operative assist in the recovery?" I asked.

"My operative is not a tactical agent. She's best when she's on her back."

My eyes narrowed as I surveyed her carefully, trying to sniff out the truth. "You planned to steal the jewel, sell it to Anatoly, then steal it back from him."

A sly smirk curled her lips. "No. I would never steal from an employer. It was an insurance policy in case of non-payment or other complications. But Anatoly didn't play straight with me. I told him I would only take the job if I was his only hire. He betrayed that trust. I feel totally justified in taking the stone from him."

"Well, if you feel justified, that's all that matters," I snarked.

She sneered at me. "I'm handing the stone to you, no strings. Take it or leave it."

I paused for a long moment. "What's the plan?"

"I've arranged transportation. We'll need weapons, ammunition, optics, and scuba gear. This is where your talent and expertise comes in."

"You want to sneak aboard the yacht, steal the jewel, and slip away under cover of darkness."

"You catch on quick."

"This is a heist."

"Yes." She smirked. "A heist to steal a precious jewel from a very bad man and return it to its rightful owner. I see nothing immoral about that."

I looked at JD. He shrugged, down for an adventure.

"Since when did you become the poster child for morality?" I asked her.

"I'm not. But you two seem to be carrying the torch."

I considered it for a moment. "I want to see the layout of Anatoly's ship."

"Not a problem."

"I'm sure he'll keep the jewel in a safe onboard. I want to know the make and model."

"Way ahead of you."

She pulled out her cell phone, launched the photos app, and zoomed in on a picture. She handed the device to me.

"That's the floor plan of Anatoly's ship."

I scrolled through several images, one for each deck. It was an 84-meter *Altoviti* with multiple decks and a helipad. A boat only a gangster or a tech billionaire could afford.

"According to my source, there is a StrongTite™ safe in a hidden compartment in the master stateroom," Lily said.

"Can you get into the safe?"

She gave me a look. "Honey, please. There isn't a lock that can keep me out."

"How did you get past the museum security? The case in particular."

She smirked. "I don't share trade secrets."

"I'm not a competitor."

"If you think I'm going to give away all my secrets on the first date, you're sadly mistaken."

"This really isn't our first date, if you think about it."

"Tristan's yacht doesn't count."

"That felt more like a third date."

Her eyes narrowed at me. "What makes you think you could have gone all the way? I'm not that easy."

"I've been known to get into a few locked boxes."

She chuckled. "I'm sure you have."

"Give me a general idea of where we're going?"

She hesitated for a moment, surveying me carefully. "South."

"And our method of travel?"

"A 59-foot racing boat. Plenty fast enough to get us there and back." That captivating smile curled her lips again. "You guys like adventure, don't you?"

I didn't answer. "You're sure the exchange is going to take place tomorrow?"

"According to my source. If anything changes, I will let you know."

I was silent for a moment as I contemplated the plan. I didn't trust her. Not for a second.

She took the last swig of her whiskey, then set the glass on the table and stood up. "Thanks for the drink, gentlemen. I take it since I'm not in handcuffs, we have an agreement?"

I looked her up and down. She was hard to say *no* to. "As long as you keep to your word, and I get the jewel back."

"I'll keep my word. I'll lead you to the jewel, and we'll get it back. I guarantee it."

"That's confidence."

"Confidence is half the game." A diabolical smirk curled her pretty lips. "I'll be in touch."

We watched her saunter away and disappear into the crowd.

"We're just going to let her walk away?" JD said.

"For now."

"Are you going to tell Jean-Claude?"

"Not yet. I think the less people that know about this, the better. Especially if this goes wrong."

We had another drink, then headed back to *Diver Down*. JD dropped me off at the dock, and I jogged to the *Avventura*.

I got a text from Lily after I took Buddy out for a quick walk. *[Care to mix a little pleasure with business?]*

## 43

"You're a professional thief, and you want me to invite you to my home? You might steal all my stuff," I said, not entirely joking.

"What's the matter? You think I might steal your heart?"

"You'd have to be pretty talented to do that."

"Trust me, I have many talents. Don't you want a chance to crack my safe?"

It was a tempting offer. I was sure I could figure out the right combination. "If you promise to behave, I'll let you come over for one drink. Then you have to go. No funny business."

"Yes, sir," she mocked.

I told her where she could find me, but I suspected she already knew.

I sat on the aft deck, petting Buddy, waiting for her to arrive, thinking this was a bad idea.

A ride-share dropped Lily off in the parking lot, and she strutted down the dock. I waved to her, and she made her way to the *Avventura* and crossed the passerelle.

Buddy barked and bounced excitedly.

Lily knelt down and petted the little terrorist. He quickly succumbed to her charms, and I began to question his judge of character.

Apparently, mine was questionable as well.

I escorted Lily into the salon. I grabbed a bottle of whiskey from behind the bar and another glass, then escorted her up to the sky deck. It was a nice place to have a drink. Stars flickered overhead, the moon glowed in the sky, reflecting on the water. It was a quiet, calm night. A gentle breeze blew through the marina. Boats swayed, and waves lapped against hulls.

"If I knew you had a Jacuzzi, I would have brought a suit."

"Suits are optional."

She gave me a sassy look. "You're not going to get into my vault that easily."

"Oh yeah? What do I have to do?"

"I'm just here for one drink, remember?"

I scoffed.

"Don't get too cocky." She paused in thought. "You know, maybe we should keep this strictly professional until we complete the job."

"Professional? Stealing a precious jewel from a Russian gangster is professional?"

"I take my work seriously."

"So do I."

"I wouldn't want you getting all emotional on me."

"Now, look who's cocky."

She shrugged. "I have certain gifts. I can't help it if men find my *personality* irresistible."

I laughed. "I think I can resist."

She sipped the whiskey, took a step closer, and looked at me with smoldering eyes. "Can you?"

Her sultry voice drifted across the night air.

Lily took another step, her eyes locked with mine. Her lips hovered tantalizingly close. Her hot breath tickled my skin. Her warm body was millimeters from mine.

Who would be the first to make a move?

The smell of whiskey mixed with her scented body wash. Her wet lips begged for attention. A collision was imminent. At the last second, she backed away, and a devious grin tugged her lips. "Maybe you're right. We shouldn't complicate things."

Now she was just playing with me.

"Tell me. Who made the first attempt on the jewel?"

"I don't know. Could have been anybody."

"Was it you?"

"Not my style. I don't go in guns blazing, and I usually work alone."

"You're working with me."

"Extenuating circumstances. Besides, I knew Jean-Claude would use a decoy. He always does. Plus, I prefer non-violence. I'm a thief, not an assassin." She thought for a moment. "It could have been Anatoly's men, attempting a brute force attack. Saves him the commission."

I stared deep into her eyes, looking for signs of deception. She didn't flinch, twitch, or look away. I had no doubt that she was a skilled liar, but I didn't figure her for that first attempt.

She finished her whiskey and dangled her empty glass. "I guess it's time for me to leave."

I grinned. "I guess so."

That wasn't the answer she was looking for. This was a game, and she wanted me to break first. There was a long, empty pause as we stared at each other. We both wanted the same thing.

"Why do you do this?" I asked.

"Why not?"

"You're a smart, talented girl. I'm sure there are many other ways you could apply yourself."

She laughed. "What are you, my guidance counselor?"

I chuckled.

"Why do you do what you do? The department sure as hell doesn't pay for this boat. Doesn't seem like you need money."

I shrugged. "Sense of personal responsibility. If we're not part of the solution, we're part of the problem."

She rolled her eyes. "Bullshit. You like the chase. And I like the thrill of not getting caught."

She inched closer again, her eyes like a predator. Her warm body pressed against mine. "It's already complicated, isn't it?" Her lips were perilously close. "What's a little more?"

Her lips melted into mine. Our tongues danced, and our hands explored each other. I traced the svelte curves of her sumptuous form. The taste of her lip gloss, the smell of her hair, the beat of her heart against my chest—it was intoxicating. The captain stood up and took notice.

She liked to live on the edge. And, I guess, so did I.

## 44

It wasn't long before her skimpy top was on the deck. The mini-skirt soon followed. Her gravity-defying peaks glowed in the pale moonlight.

Her skin was soft and smooth. The pulse of desire pounded in my heart. My fingers slipped underneath her panties, and I slid them over her delightful hips. They tumbled down her toned thighs to the deck.

Her fingers fumbled around my waistband, and soon my shorts joined the rest of her ensemble. I peeled off my shirt, and we tumbled our way onto a sun pad.

Our hips collided, her legs wrapped tight around me. Her breathy moans filled my ear and echoed across the marina. The moon and stars were our audience, and we gave them a helluva show.

I guess I had the right combination to the safe.

We wore ourselves out on the sun pad, then retired to my stateroom on the bridge deck. I dipped back into the vault again one more time for good measure.

By the time we were finished, my heart was pounding, and I was breathing heavily. Lily curled beside me, nuzzling up. I passed out with a head full of whiskey and pleasure chemicals. As long as she didn't steal my dog, it would be okay.

The morning came too soon. Sunlight blasted through the cracks in the blinds. I peeled a sleepy eye open and reached a hand to feel empty sheets beside me.

It wasn't a surprise. I didn't figure she'd stick around. But the smell of coffee and bacon caught me off guard.

I climbed out of bed, pulled on a pair of shorts, and stumbled down to the galley. Lily slaved over the grill wearing one of my T-shirts and a pair of boxers.

"I'm borrowing this, by the way. Not stealing."

I chuckled.

She looked just as good wearing my clothes as she did all dolled up in a mini-skirt and stilettos. There was definitely something sexy about it.

"I didn't figure you for the domestic type," I said.

"I love a good breakfast as much as the next girl. Besides, it's hard to screw up scrambled eggs and bacon."

I poured a cup of coffee while she dished up the goods. We took a seat at the settee, and I sipped my coffee and crunched on crispy bacon.

"Where does this all end for you?"

She gave me a quizzical look. "Me and you? Or this lifestyle of mine?"

I chuckled. "The lifestyle."

She shrugged. "A few more big scores, then I take my little nest egg and disappear in some quiet corner of the world that's sunny and has nice beaches."

"Most thieves I know have retired to a cozy corner in a 6x8 cell."

She rolled her eyes playfully. "Don't be such a downer. I haven't been caught yet. And if you were going to arrest me, you'd have already done it by now."

"You cross me, and I will take you down."

"I would expect nothing less."

"So, what's the next big score?"

"After we get the jewel back? I don't know." A sly smirk curled her delightful lips. "And even if I did know, I wouldn't tell you."

"As long as it doesn't happen in Coconut Key, I really don't care."

"I can't imagine you not caring."

"It's not that I don't care, but there are limits to what I can do."

"Why here? Why Coconut Key?"

"Is there a better place to be? This is home. My friends are here. The people I care about."

"It's a nice place, I'll give you that."

I paused. "Are you familiar with the scorpion and the frog?"

Lily smiled. "Ah, yes. The scorpion wants to get across the river and hitches a ride on the frog's back. The frog's worried the scorpion will sting him. But the scorpion assures the frog he won't because they'd both die since the scorpion can't swim."

"And how does the fable end?"

"They both die. The scorpion stings the frog because it's in his nature."

I gave her a long look.

"I'm not a scorpion."

"Just remember, they both died."

"Well, I like to live." She smiled.

We finished breakfast, and I helped Lily clean up. She sauntered up to the sky deck, gathered her clothes, and got dressed in my stateroom.

She gave me a kiss on the cheek before leaving. "I'll be in touch when I have confirmation about the exchange. I'm thinking we should leave for the rendezvous point in the late afternoon. That should give us plenty of time."

"Want to tell me where we're going?"

"90 miles, Deputy," she said with a smile. "90 miles."

We were going to Cuba.

I escorted her through the salon and pulled open the door. Buddy bounced and barked, and she knelt down and petted him before leaving.

She gave me another kiss on the cheek, then sauntered across the passerelle. I watched from the aft deck as she strolled to the parking lot and hopped into a ride-share.

Daniels called not long after. "Looks like Commissioner Johnson wants to talk."

"That's surprising."

"He's in the hospital right now. Got the shit kicked out of him last night. Altercation with his cellmate. Get to the hospital and see what he has to say."

"We're on our way."

I ended the call and dialed JD. He swung by the marina, and we headed to Coconut General in the Porsche. We pushed through the sea-foam green hallways to the nurses' station. The charge nurse directed us to the commissioner's room.

We stepped inside. Dario was asleep. Shafts of sunlight cut through the blinds, and a muted TV flickered. His wrist was cuffed to the bedrail.

The commissioner was battered and bruised. Purple circles rimmed his eyes, and his nose had been broken. He suffered a few cracked ribs and was on supplemental oxygen for good measure.

Dario stirred as we stepped to the bed.

"I hear you've got something to say."

"I can't go back there. You can't put me back in that place. It's filled with savages." His speech was weak, and his breath labored.

"You should have thought of that before you started taking bribes and having staff members killed."

"I didn't have anyone killed. I'll name everybody involved. But I can't do time."

"Tell me everything you know, and I'll talk to the state attorney."

"I want a deal first. If I tell you what I know, I lose my leverage. I didn't get where I am by giving up leverage."

"Where you are is not an enviable position." I paused. "Look, we know Maverick was kicking back funds to you in exchange for your vote. What I need is a paper trail. And I need to know who shot up the Frisky Kitty."

"I had nothing to do with that. I didn't know they would do that. I just mentioned that Crosby had threatened to go public if I didn't pay him."

"And you didn't think they would take matters into their own hands?"

"They'd never gotten violent before."

"Tell me about their operation."

"There are three of them. Maverick, a girl who I think he's got something going on with, and a guy in his late 20s."

"What do you know about them?"

"I know Maverick's real name is Milton. He's from Texas."

"You know his last name?"

"Fox."

"What about the money trail?"

After some hemming and hawing, Dario detailed the ins-and-outs of the kickbacks. JD's theory was pretty spot on.

We left the hospital, and I called Denise. Her fingers tapped the keys as she ran background information on Milton Fox. "He's got outstanding warrants in Texas for fraud, bribery, and a host of other charges. Looks like he was pulling the same scams there. He was arrested with two co-conspirators, Luke Everett and Karen Grant. I'll text you their information."

I ended the call, and a moment later, several images buzzed my phone.

Maverick, a.k.a. Milton Fox, was in his mid 30s. He was bald on top with brown hair trimmed short on the sides. He had a square face, narrow brown eyes, and a permanent 5 o'clock shadow. He was 5'8" and stocky. A definite possibility for the Frisky Kitty shooter.

Luke Everett was in his late 20s with short curly blonde hair and green eyes. He had a prominent lower jaw and a slight underbite. Even in his mug shot, he had a cocky grin.

Karen Gates was early 30s with *resting bitch-face*. The corners of her mouth angled downward, creating a permanent frown. Her blonde hair was pulled back into a ponytail for her mug-shot, and her heavy eyeliner was smudged. Her brown roots were showing. She'd probably shed a few tears during her initial arrest and bawled in the back of the patrol car on the way down to the station.

We had a warrant in no time and were at Maverick's door in Stingray Bay with a tactical team. The expensive cars were still in the driveway. There was a 42-foot sport-fish in the canal behind the house.

"Coconut County!" I shouted, banging on the front door.

Erickson and Faulkner waited eagerly with a battering ram.

Mendoza and Robinson had circled around back.

Curious neighbors gawked through blinds at the swarm of deputies surrounding the posh estate.

There was no response.

I nodded to Erickson and Faulkner. They heaved the ram against the mahogany door, turning it into scrap. Wood splintered, and frosted glass shattered. Chards danced on the Italian marble. The door swung wide.

I tossed in a flash-bang grenade. It bounced across the marble and thundered to life in the living room, marring the hardwoods.

We stormed into the foyer, weapons in the firing position. The barrel of my pistol swept the corners, angling up the spiral staircase to the second floor.

The barrel of an assault rifle angled around a 2nd-floor corner and aimed over the balustrade.

Muzzle flash flickered, and the foyer filled with a deafening clatter as bullets peppered the expensive tile.

## 45

I dashed for cover and returned fire. My pistol hammered against my palm, and smoke wafted from the barrel.

Bullets crisscrossed the air.

Sheetrock exploded with molten copper, spraying plumes of gypsum and dust.

The tangy scent of gunpowder drifted about as smoke hazed the vaulted foyer.

The exchange lasted a few seconds, but it seemed longer. There was a thump as the shooter fell to the ground, and the weapon clattered away.

Mendoza and Robinson had breached the rear door and advanced into the living room, clearing the kitchen along the way. They announced themselves as they approached the foyer and held up at a hallway that led to a guest bedroom and half bath.

JD took the lead, sprinting up the staircase to the second-floor landing where Luke Everett lay in a pool of blood.

Jack kicked the weapon out of reach for good measure, then held up at the corner and peered down a hallway, looking for threats.

Erickson and Faulkner were right behind him. Faulkner knelt down and felt for a pulse, but Luke was gone.

I brought up the rear.

There was a bedroom just off the landing. Faulkner and Erickson took a position on either side. We covered the long hallway to the master bedroom while they kicked open the door and cleared the guest bedroom. They searched the closet, the bathroom, checked under the bed, then made their way back into the hall.

Mendoza and Robinson kept an eye on things downstairs.

The rotor blades of Tango One pattered overhead as it circled the house.

I shouted down the hallway, "Put your weapons down and come out with your hands up. Let's not make things any worse than they already are."

There was no response, but I heard a floorboard creak beyond the door to the master bedroom.

We readied our weapons.

My heart thumped my chest, and my ears still rang from the clatter of gunfire in the foyer. Adrenaline spiked my veins.

Halfway down the hall, there was a door to the right that I assumed was another guest bedroom. The door on the left was perhaps a storage closet.

We crept forward to the guest bedroom. Erickson and Faulkner kept their weapons aimed at the master while JD and I breached the second guest room. The door flung wide, and we swung our barrels inside and cleared the corners. A queen bed was the focal point. The sheets were unmade, and a half-filled roller suitcase lay atop the bed. Sun beamed in through two windows, one on either side. There was a dresser, a mirror, and a small office area with a desk and a chair. A large flatscreen was mounted to the wall, and there was a video game console with wireless controllers.

The room, the attached bath, and the closet were clear.

We slipped back into the hallway, then cleared the storage closet on the left side of the corridor.

We continued toward the master bedroom. I cringed as I stepped on a squeaky floorboard.

Gunfire erupted.

Bullets punched through the cheap particle board door. As expensive as these houses were, the construction was shoddy.

I flattened myself against the wall as bullets rocketed down the hallway.

One caught Faulkner in the chest.

It spun him around and dropped him to the floor with an agonizing groan. The thud shook the floor.

I returned fire, blasting at the door.

So did JD.

Erickson knelt beside Faulkner to render aid.

There was no blood.

The vest had saved him. But he'd taken a hit to the collarbone. His face twisted with pain. Even with a vest, it's like taking a sledgehammer to the chest. Never a good feeling.

Bits of particleboard and paint fluttered from the door as molten copper continued to spray.

We waited until the perp on the other side needed to reload.

The clatter went silent a moment, and JD kicked the door open.

Maverick slapped another cartridge into his AR 15.

I squeezed the trigger.

So did JD.

We filled him full of holes before he could hit the bolt catch and chamber another round.

His body jerked and twitched with each hit. He tumbled back and fell to the carpet, oozing blood.

I advanced around the king-size bed.

Karen crouched behind the mattress by the nightstand. She dropped her pistol and raised her hands in the air. "Don't shoot. Don't shoot!"

She looked up at me with terrified eyes, trembling.

I kicked the weapon away. "Face down. Hands behind your head!"

Karen complied, and I pounced on her back and ratcheted the cuffs around her wrists.

There were half-packed suitcases on the bed, just like the guest room. Looked like they were preparing to make a getaway.

Tango One still circled.

I yanked Karen to her feet and dragged her out of the bedroom. She wept as I pulled her down the hallway. She had a grim, terrified look on her face as she stared at the fallen bodies of her comrades. We tried not to step in blood, but it was almost impossible.

The upscale neighborhood of Stingray Bay wasn't exactly used to this kind of activity. Curious neighbors gathered as more deputies arrived. Red and blues flashed. Soon, the scene swarmed with first responders and medical personnel. The red and white lights of an ambulance flickered. Brenda and her crew arrived along with the forensic team.

I stuffed Karen into the back of a patrol car.

"You're keeping me in business," Brenda said as she passed.

I followed her inside, and Dietrich went to work, snapping photos of the gruesome scene. Forensic investigators marked and cataloged every shell casing and bullet hole.

We found several kilos of cocaine and a fat stack of cash in a guest bedroom closet. It seemed like fraud and murder weren't the only things Maverick and his crew were into.

Paris Delaney was on scene with her news crew by the time the bodies had been bagged. The camera soaked up footage of the dead perps being wheeled out on gurneys and placed into the medical examiner's van. She approached with her crew as I stepped outside. The lens was in my face, and the cameraman pulled focus. The fluffy little boom mic hovered overhead.

"Deputy Wild, can you confirm the rumors that these individuals were responsible for the Frisky Kitty shooting and the deaths of the two staffers in Commissioner Johnson's office?"

"I'll wait until we have all the evidence analyzed before I comment."

"That's not a *no*," she said with a smirk.

After we wrapped up at the scene, JD and I made our way to the Porsche and headed back to the station. We filled out after-action reports, then had a chat with Karen Grant in the interrogation room.

"Who was the nightclub shooter?" I asked.

"It wasn't me. I didn't have anything to do with it. It was all Maverick's doing. I swear."

Her answer didn't surprise me. "You were just along for the ride, right?"

"I swear, I didn't know what he had done until after he did it."

"You could have come forward. That makes you an accessory after the fact."

Her eyes narrowed at me. "What are you going to charge me with? I didn't do anything."

I laughed. "That's a good one."

"I pleaded with him to turn himself in."

"I'm sure you did. You just happened to have a weapon during a shootout with the police."

"He gave me the gun and told me to stay down and hide by the bed. What was I supposed to do? I didn't shoot anybody."

I couldn't say for sure who really pulled the trigger at the nightclub. It could have been Maverick. It could have been Luke. Either way, Karma caught up with them. And I suspected Karen would do a long stint. When and *if* she was done doing Florida time, she'd get sent to Texas to serve out her sentence for the previous crimes she had committed there.

Karen broke into sobs as we left. She wasn't crying out of remorse or guilt. She was crying because she got caught.

As per protocol, we had to surrender our duty weapons and would need to go through the standard psychological evaluation. Our little covert mission, planned for this evening, to recover the jewel would have to be completely off the books.

Normally, it would be time for a drink. But we both needed to stay frosty.

Daniels caught up with us in the hallway. "You making any progress on the jewel heist?"

I hesitated for a long moment.

## 46

"We have some promising leads," I said. "I'll keep you posted."

His suspicious eyes surveyed me.

I felt terrible keeping him out of the loop. But I didn't want to risk saying anything. The walls had ears around here.

We left the station and grabbed something to eat at *Five Fathoms*. It was an upscale surf and turf restaurant. We figured we had earned a good meal, and I enjoyed a nice filet topped with lobster.

I called Isabella and told her about my little covert op with Lily.

"You're insane."

"Jack's the crazy one. Not me."

"I'm not so sure about that."

"Look, we get in, steal the jewel, get out, and return it to its rightful owner. Everyone's happy."

"Except for Anatoly. That guy is bad news. You need to be careful."

"That's why I need your help."

She said nothing.

"The method may be questionable, but the cause is just. It's a good deed."

"No good deed goes unpunished."

I asked flatly, "Can I count on your support?"

She sighed. "What do you need from me?"

We discussed the ins and outs of the mission.

After the meal, we went back to the *Avventura* and prepped our gear.

Jack had acquired a lot of handy toys—Draeger rebreathers, night vision optics with infrared, a high-powered sniper rifle, smoke canisters, and even a few hand grenades. I didn't know where he got some of the stuff, and I didn't want to know. We also had an RPG-7 we'd acquired during a bust.

I grabbed another pistol, press checked it, loaded my pockets with extra magazines, and grabbed my short-barreled AR with suppressor as well.

The amber ball was nearing the horizon, speckling the water with highlights. The sky was a mix of pink and blue as the setting sun painted the fluffy clouds.

Lily showed up to the marina in a stunning 59-foot matte black *Apex X600* racing boat. With six outboard engines, it made a whopping 2,700 hp. It was the ultimate luxury racing boat. A performance icon. The benchmark by which all others were measured. A true predator.

There was a fore and aft lounge with red hand-stitched seating. The fit and finish oozed luxury and comfort. Precise engineering provided a low center of gravity and excellent performance. A 4-pillar carbon fiber hardtop and a tempered safety glass windscreen offered protection from the elements at the helm station. Dual, flush-mounted multifunction displays placed control and information at your fingertips. The meticulous design was crafted with titanium, carbon fiber, and composite materials. Bow and stern thrusters let you get into and out of tight spots with ease. An advanced gyro-stabilizer eliminated 90% of the roll. There were plenty of forward-facing bolstered seats. Integrated lighting created the perfect ambience, and the BTX stereo kept the party pumping.

The cabin was the perfect place to escape the hot sun, appointed with premium Italian leather and a high-low TV. It included a queen berth, a molded-in sofa, and hull side windows and skylights. There was a luxury day head with a shower. A 14-foot beam offered plenty of space. The thousand-gallon fuel capacity was perfect for these long trips.

It was the epitome of performance and style.

JD's eyes rounded when he saw the sleek craft, green with envy. "Now, this is nice!"

"You steal this?" I asked.

Lily just looked at me and laughed.

We loaded the gear aboard the boat and set off on our journey. With Lily at the helm, she idled out of the marina, then throttled up, bringing the beast on plane.

It was fast.

Real fast.

The engines howled, spitting a rooster tail as we skimmed across the surface, bouncing on the swells. With good weather and calm seas, we could get to Cuba in the blink of an eye.

The wind swirled, and saltwater sprayed.

The weather was great for the time being. Just a little light chop. Hopefully, it would hold, but there was some nasty weather out there, according to reports.

The sun dipped below the horizon, and the sky turned gray, then midnight blue. It wasn't long before the moon presided over the sea, and the stars flickered. Perhaps they looked upon us like fools.

Entering Cuban waters was illegal without a permit from the Coast Guard. You risked having your boat confiscated and faced fines and penalties, and potentially up to 10 years imprisonment. Currently, you could only get a permit with an application accompanied by an approved special license from the Department of Commerce.

We didn't have any of that.

## 47

The US recognizes Cuban waters extending 12 miles offshore. We found Anatoly's yacht within that zone. I had no doubt that he had some arrangement with the Cuban authorities.

We hadn't run into any trouble on the way down. The Coast Guard didn't stop us. There were no helicopters hovering in the air. My guess was that coming back we might encounter more resistance. A Go-Fast boat hauling ass in the middle of the night usually warrants attention.

We kept our distance from the superyacht. Lily killed the engine, and we drifted on the inky swells. The waves lapped against the hull. The boat pitched and rolled with a gentle motion.

I surveyed the yacht with infrared from the forward lounge. The boat was massive. The pinnacle of luxury. The name *Escape* was painted across the stern in gold metallic.

We were half a mile out. Far enough to avoid detection unless someone was really looking.

JD kept watch of the surrounding seas. Drifting with the swells without running lights in the pitch blackness can be dangerous.

"You're sure everything is on schedule?" I asked Lily.

"I'm positive. Just be patient."

We waited for about 30 minutes, and nothing happened. Then, the distant patter of rotor blades thumped across the sky. At first, I was a little concerned we might be in for trouble.

Lily checked the time. "That's Le Grand."

A small black helicopter with a shrouded tail rotor zipped across the sky. It circled the superyacht, then made an approach from the starboard side. Since the seas were calm, the pilot had a fairly easy time touching down on the helipad.

The rotors spun down, and the passenger door slid open. Charles Le Grand hopped out on the foredeck, carrying a small aluminum briefcase.

Anatoly appeared with two goons to greet the thief.

From what I could tell, there were at least eight security personnel on board. Lily's informant reclined in the forward lounge. Annabelle sipped a cocktail on a chez lounge near a white grand piano, watching the transaction take place through massive forward windows that encircled the compartment.

I had seen a few crew members. There was no doubt a captain, an engineer, an executive chef, and several deck-hands were aboard.

From the body language, I could tell the exchange with Le Grand was tense. These kinds of transactions always are. Anatoly wanted to see the jewel, and Le Grand wanted to see the money. But by this time, he'd already given up his leverage. He was on the deck of Anatoly's boat in Cuban waters.

Le Grand handed the case to Anatoly. The Russian gangster dialed the combination, flipped the latches, and opened the case. He surveyed the gem for a moment. It looked like he shined a flashlight on it. Satisfied, he nodded to his goon, who tossed a duffel bag of cash onto the deck.

Le Grand never lost eye contact with the goon as he knelt down to pick up the bag. He unzipped it, glanced inside for a moment, and surveyed the contents. I'm assuming there were stacks of cash, but I couldn't see from this angle.

Le Grand seemed pleased.

The parties exchanged a brief nod, and Le Grand turned and walked back to the helicopter, the rotors still spinning.

That's when Anatoly's goon drew a pistol from a shoulder holster. Two flashes erupted from the barrel. The bullets drilled into Le Grand's back, spitting geysers of blood. He collapsed on the deck, his spine severed. His body twitched momentarily, and crimson pooled.

"Nice guy," I said.

"Another reason why I don't feel bad about screwing Anatoly over," Lily said. "He probably would have killed me."

"Maybe Le Grand did you a favor."

"It would appear so."

The helicopter pilot spun down the blades.

Anatoly turned around and walked into the forward lounge through sliding doors. He had a few brief words with the blonde, who seemed a little stunned, but maintained her cool. She asked to see the jewel, and Anatoly obliged.

He opened the case and took out the precious gem. Anatoly marveled at it for a moment, then handed it to Annabelle.

Her eyes sparkled almost as much as the jewel. She stood up, wrapped her arms around his neck, and planted a wet kiss on his sour mug.

When the two broke from their embrace, Annabelle handed the gangster the jewel. He placed it back into the case and disappeared into a passageway.

Anatoly's goons hefted Le Grand's body from the deck and tossed him over the gunwale. He splashed into the water below—shark bait. A goon called for a deckhand to clean up the mess.

The crew knew who they worked for. It was no secret. I'm sure they were compensated handsomely.

The helicopter pilot climbed out of the sleek black aircraft and had a few words with the goons. Then they all marched down the side deck, descended the steps, and entered amidships to the receiving lobby. I lost sight of them after that.

"You ready to go to work?" Lily asked.

---

## 48

L ily and I did last-minute safety checks and donned the dive gear—black masks, black fins, black suits. JD would stay aboard the boat as overwatch. There was no way I would leave that to Lily. She might take off and leave us.

"You sure you can handle this?" I asked.

"I'm no Navy SEAL, but I'm strong in the water. I can manage this swim," Lily assured.

We fell into the inky swells. I cleared my mask and finned just below the surface. It was like swimming through shoe polish.

The rebreathers didn't emit bubbles. They were closed-circuit systems that filtered carbon dioxide from exhaled air. They were good to depths of roughly 70 feet. No one would see us coming if we stayed more than a few feet under the surface. All things considered, this was an easy swim for me. I'd done this kind of thing hundreds of times before in much more difficult conditions. But even for the experienced, the open ocean at night can be daunting. Anything is possible. Anything can go wrong.

We pulled through the water, heading toward the superyacht. I kept a watch on my swim buddy. For better or worse, we were on this mission together. We were each other's lifeline.

The rays of the full moon pierced the surface of the water as the clouds parted. The running lights of the yacht made it a relatively easy target to hit.

It wasn't too long before we surfaced at the swim platform and hugged the hull. We slipped the rebreathers off, and I looped a cord through them and attached them to the lowest rung on the swim ladder below the surface. We had prepared a few different exfiltration routes. Ideally, we'd leave the way we came, undetected.

I heard footsteps above on the aft deck, and I smelled the faint traces of a cigarette wafting through the air. Smoking is terrible when on night watch. Not only does it give away your position, but it also affects night vision, and the smoke can obstruct your view.

A few moments later, the smoker tossed the cigarette over the gunwale. It flicked overhead, and the cherry flew off just before it hit the water. The footsteps marched away, and the sliding glass doors of the main deck salon opened.

I climbed onto the swim platform and drained the barrel of my short-barreled AR 15. Water ran down my legs and dripped on the swim platform.

I helped Lily aboard, then put in a wireless earbud which was paired with my satellite burner phone. I was able to have encrypted comms with Isabella through a proprietary app. I whispered, "Bravo one, Almighty, do you copy, over?"

A moment later, "Copy."

"It's nice to hear your voice."

"I don't have satellite visuals. You guys are going in blind."

"Copy."

I launched a network sniffing app which searched for the router on the boat. It gave me the IP address, which I passed on to Isabella. "Do you think you can hack the network?"

"Given enough time and determination, I can hack anything."

"Time is not our friend."

"It never is."

A boat like the *Escape* had state-of-the-art security. Multiple shipboard cameras fed an app that could be monitored on a phone or iPad, or routed to a security screen.

We crept up the molded-in stairs and crouched low below the aft deck. There was a lounge, a wet bar with fixed barstools, and a small black-domed security camera mounted on the molded-in sunshade. I didn't know if anyone was monitoring the feeds, but I didn't want to take any chances.

"I'm in," Isabella said, her voice crackling in my ear. "I accessed the network through a Wi-Fi printer with poor security protocols."

"I knew you could figure it out. Can you interrupt the camera feeds?"

"I can drop them out momentarily. If I shut them down completely, it might draw suspicion."

"Do you have access to all the feeds?"

"I do. I'll coach you through the ship."

I looked at Lily.

She nodded.

"We're ready. Say the word."

Isabella hesitated a moment. "Go!"

We climbed onto the aft deck and crouched low, hustling to the wet bar, then to the stairs that led to the bridge deck aft.

Isabella dropped the camera feed momentarily.

We left a trail of wet footprints that would give away our presence. I hoped they dried before anybody returned to the aft deck.

## 49

T his boat was designed for leisure and entertainment. Everything about it was extravagant. The fit and finish were second to none.

The bridge deck aft was home to another lounge area and a bar. Sliding glass doors opened to a full-beam master stateroom with a California king. Another domed security camera hung from the molded-in sunshade.

Isabella dropped the feed to this camera, and we scurried across the deck, slid open the door, and stepped into the stateroom.

It was opulent.

Silk carpet, the finest appointments, handcrafted wood paneling. A flatscreen display folded down from the ceiling, and there was an office area and a lounge to starboard. A Cézanne hung on the bulkhead.

The bookshelf in the office was a doorway to a secret lounge. Lily's informant had told us where we could find the compartment. We padded across the silk carpet, pulled open the bookshelf, and stepped inside.

It was a cozy room with intricate golden wood paneling. There was a chair, a small wooden end table, more bookshelves, and drawers. Against the port wall, a Picasso hung in a golden frame.

The Picasso was definitely fake.

It was on a hinge, and I swung it open to reveal a safe.

Lily examined the small vault.

"Now that we're here, I sure hope you can get into it," I whispered.

"Trust me. I got this."

The StrongTite™ safe was touted as one of the most secure on the market. It was made of a high-tech composite alloy that was 10 times stronger than steel. It had a keypad on the door with three LED status indicators—red, yellow, and green. To the left of the keypad was an access handle.

The downfall of consumer products is that schematics and designs are readily available online.

Lily pulled out a 7-inch long segment of a coat hanger she had snipped. She brandished it with a grin. "I have a special tool."

She used the straight end of the coat hanger to punch out one of the small LED lights above the keypad. Then, with the curved end, she threaded it through the hole and fumbled around until she found the solenoid. She depressed it, and the latch unlocked.

A proud grin curled on her face. "Like taking candy from a baby."

She swung the door of the *impenetrable* safe open in less than 30 seconds.

The Jewel of Aphrodite sparkled within.

All we had to do was take it and get out unnoticed.

Lily's eyes rounded as she snatched the jewel, transfixed by it. She gazed at it like a junky looks at heroin.

I held out my palm and whispered, "Give it here."

She scowled at me playfully and pulled the jewel away. "I can admire it, can't I?"

"Not here. Not now."

She frowned but slapped it into my palm.

I examined the jewel carefully for a moment, then slipped it into a zippered pouch in my suit.

Footsteps shuffled into the stateroom.

My heart spiked, filling my ears with a deafening pulse. We stood still, hesitant to even breathe.

There was no security camera angle in the master stateroom. Isabella couldn't tell me what was going on outside of the hidden compartment.

We waited for a few moments as somebody futzed around the stateroom, then used the en suite. The heavy footsteps and grunts and groans had to belong to Anatoly.

I kept my weapon ready, just in case he came into the hidden compartment.

Fortunately, after he'd taken care of business, he stepped out of the en suite and left the stateroom. His footsteps faded down a forward passageway.

I exchanged a glance with Lily, and we both breathed a sigh of relief.

We waited another moment before pushing open the hidden door. I peered through the crack and surveyed the compartment before stepping back into the stateroom.

Just as we did, Isabella crackled in my ear. "You've got company. Someone is coming up the aft steps to the bridge deck."

Footsteps rumbled.

We hustled out of the stateroom into a forward passageway. The floor was marble. Custom black design elements framed the tiles. Cream wood paneling lined the walls, and ornate wall sconces illuminated the corridor.

No expense was spared in the construction of the boat.

We crept forward toward another closed door and held up. I carefully cracked it open and peered into the next passageway.

It was empty.

We slipped through the door and pulled it shut behind us, then made our way toward a central staircase with a silver baluster that spiraled above and below.

On the other side of the staircase was another passage that led to more guest rooms and the forward lounge with the piano. Anatoly's deep voice rumbled from within the lounge, speaking with Annabelle.

"How is your friend getting off the boat?" I whispered.

"The same way she got on."

Our conversation was cut short when a goon spiraled down the steps. His eyes widened when he saw us. He drew his pistol and took aim.

## 50

———

My rifle hammered against my shoulder as I squeezed the trigger. The suppressor muffled the sound slightly, but not enough. Smoke wafted, and the smell of gunpowder filled my nostrils.

My bullets smacked the goon's chest with a wet thud. Crimson blood spattered, and he twisted around, falling back against the baluster. He groaned and tried to suck in a breath, but his lungs were pulverized.

He bounced off the handrail, then tumbled down the steps and face-planted at the base of the stairs. Blood oozed from the caverns in his chest, seeping onto the expensive tile.

The game was on.

Our mission was covert no longer.

Commotion filled the passageway behind us as we plunged down the spiral staircase to the main deck lobby.

Goons approached from either side of the staircase.

I took aim aft, while Lily took aim forward.

I squeezed off several rounds, peppering the thug advancing toward me. He tumbled back against the bulkhead, staining it with blood as he slid to the tile.

Lily's goon suffered the same fate. The girl could shoot—there was no doubt about it.

Another thug burst into the aft passageway from the salon. He aimed his pistol and squeezed the trigger. Muzzle flash flickered, and bullets rocketed down the corridor.

We continued to spiral our way down, below deck, to the crew quarters. With a few twists and turns, we found ourselves in a port-side passageway, heading aft toward the beach club/garage.

Heavy footsteps of goons were right behind us.

We sprinted down the corridor at a frantic pace. I opened the hatch to the garage and pushed inside as two more goons rounded the corner behind us. They opened fire just as I shut the hatch and locked it.

The bullets pinged off the metal door.

My heart punched my chest, and adrenaline coursed through my veins.

The yacht had a drive-in tender, accessible through a port-side door. The garage was filled with jet skis and water toys. A small davit allowed easy deployment into the water. Beyond the tender was a bar and lounge area. The rear garage door could be opened, giving access to the swim platform.

Bullets continued to smash the hatch.

"Open the garage," I shouted to Lily.

When I turned around, she had her weapon aimed at me.

I groaned. I should have known better.

"Sorry, Tyson. It's in my nature. Give me the stone."

"I don't think you've thought this through."

"I've thought it through. Let's not make this complicated. I like you. I really do. I don't want to hurt you. Just give me the stone. Now."

I made a slight movement.

She got twitchy. "Put the weapon down! Slowly and carefully."

I unslung the weapon from my shoulder and carefully set it on the deck.

"Now your sidearm. Thumb and index finger only."

I complied.

Anatoly's goons banged on the hatch, trying to access it. But it was locked from within. It wouldn't take them long to access the compartment from another entry point.

"Now the gem," Lily demanded.

I unzipped the pouch, pulled out the sparkling ruby, and tossed it to her.

She had to take her left hand from the rifle to catch it. When she did, I thought about making a move. But that barrel looked awfully intimidating, and her aim was pretty good.

She slipped the jewel into a pocket, then backed away. She opened the port-side garage door, boarded the tender and cranked up the engines.

Exhaust filled the compartment.

"I'm gonna laugh if you run out of gas halfway back to the Keys."

She looked at the gauge. "It's got a full tank."

Lily throttled up and launched out of the garage, into the open ocean. The outboards howled as she disappeared into the night, spitting white water.

Gunfire erupted from the main deck.

I assumed a few goons were taking potshots at her.

I scooped my weapons from the deck, sprinted across the garage, and slipped into the water. I figured I could swim under the boat to the starboard side where the rebreathers were. I could hold my breath a long time. Not *freediver long*, but long enough.

I swam out of the garage into the choppy sea on the port side. The swells had grown more intense, and the wind had picked up.

Goons on the main deck above angled pistols over the gunwale and opened fire. Muzzle flash flickered in the night, and bullets plunked into the water.

I dove down, pulling myself under the bottom of the boat. I swam across the centerline in the inky blackness, the running lights of the boat providing enough illumination to navigate.

I pulled hard, my chest thumping, my lungs beginning to burn. When I reached the starboard side of the swim platform, I noticed the rebreathers were gone.

Somebody must have found them.

A goon plummeted down the aft steps toward the swim platform. He aimed his pistol at me and fired off a few rounds. The barrel flashed, and smoke wafted.

I dove below as bullets plunked into the water around me.

The situation wasn't looking good.

Under the water, I heard the rumble of an engine. The deep V-hull of the tender carved through the water, heading toward me.

More gunshots erupted.

The muffled sounds and flashes filtered through the water.

I heard a thud, then the goon on the swim platform fell into the water, blood seeping from his wounds. His empty eyes stared into the abyss.

I surfaced and sucked in a breath of air just as Lily pulled alongside the superyacht.

"Get in!"

She didn't have to tell me twice. I swam to the stern and used the ladder to climb aboard while Lily blasted at goons on the aft deck of the superyacht. They fired over the gunwale at the tender.

Bullets popped and pinged, smacking fiberglass.

As soon as I cleared the transom, Lily throttled up and banked the boat around. The engine screamed, spitting a frothy wake. Wind swirled as we bounced across the swells.

I gave myself a quick once over to make sure I wasn't hit, then looked back at the superyacht as it grew smaller.

Bullets continued to snap through the air until we were out of range.

"Didn't think you were coming back," I said.

"Yeah, well, I seem to have developed a conscience."

"That's not a bad thing."

"It is in my line of work."

We plowed through the abyss and met up with JD aboard the *Apex*. We transferred to the speed boat, leaving the tender behind.

JD throttled up and headed north. The six outboards roared, and we skimmed across the surface.

"What the hell was that?" JD asked with an annoyed face.

Lily shrugged. "All part of the plan."

His skeptical eyes narrowed at her. "You get the jewel?"

Lily grinned.

"Speaking of," I said. "Hand it over."

She made a pouty face. "Don't I get a little something for coming back?"

"Isn't a clean conscience enough?"

She rolled her eyes, dug into a zippered pouch on her suit, and retrieved the gem. She placed it in my palm and clasped my hand tight. "You're sure Jean-Claude deserves this?"

"Matters not. I took a job to protect the stone. Then to see its safe return."

I took the priceless ruby and secured it in my pocket. I didn't know if it had mystical powers, and I didn't care.

We zipped away into the night, heading toward international waters. I was just starting to relax, thinking we got away clean, when I heard the sound of rotor blades in the distance.

I grabbed the infrared optics and scanned the sky. The small black helicopter streaked above the surface of the ocean, barreling toward us.

"Incoming," I shouted.

The racing boat scorched across the water as fast as we could go, given the conditions. The swells grew higher as a storm rolled in our direction. It wasn't an optimal situation.

Soon, the helicopter was right on our tail.

At the stern, I shouldered my rifle and took aim.

A goon hung out of the passenger side door and opened fire. Flashes flickered from the barrel.

I squeezed my trigger in rapid succession. The rifle hammered against my shoulder. Hot brass ejected from the port, chiming against the deck. I crouched low at the stern and aimed at the glass windshield, trying to take out the pilot.

The helicopter caught up and buzzed alongside us. The door gunner unleashed a torrent of copper.

Bullets crisscrossed the night.

They snapped past my ears and tore up the fiberglass hull, and put holes in handcrafted seats.

The helicopter circled around.

Anatoly was on board.

The pilot swooped by, making another pass.

More bullets crisscrossed.

The bolt locked. I pressed the mag release button, and the magazine fell away. I jammed another one in, hit the bolt catch, and kept firing.

It was a symphony of chaos—the roar of the engine, the report of the gun, the pounding of rotor blades, the wind whistling my ears.

The boat skipped across the swells, making accuracy difficult.

Saltwater splashed and sprayed.

The helicopter buzzed around, and the door gunner started aiming at the engines instead of us. We'd be much easier targets if we were dead in the water.

The helicopter paced along the port side. Bullets popped and pinged off the engine cover. After a few lucky hits, smoke billowed from the engine. It sputtered, then died. Flames erupted, rippling in the wind.

JD hit the fuel cutoff.

Lily grabbed the fire extinguisher and doused the flames while I kept firing at the helicopter.

They circled around again.

I emptied the second magazine, then reached for the big gun. The RPG-7. I unscrewed the safety on the grenade, shouldered the weapon, and took aim.

I only had one shot. The black helicopter circled around behind us, making its profile slim.

With the craft lined up in my iron sights, I pulled the trigger. The booster charge launched the grenade from the tube, blowing a blinding flash of exhaust out of the rear.

After 10 meters, the rocket motor ignited and propelled the grenade through the night sky.

The pilot veered the helicopter, and the grenade soared past the craft, disappearing into the abyss.

My one shot missed.

I tossed the launcher to the deck, picked up my AR, and slapped in a fresh magazine.

The helicopter hung back for a moment, the pilot a little gun shy now.

He veered to port and pulled alongside us again. The goon at the door unleashed another flurry of bullets.

The copper devils snapped through the air, smacking the hull again.

We all crouched low.

Lily and I returned fire.

One of my bullets caught the door gunner in the chest. He flopped back into his seat, blood gushing. His weapon tumbled away and smacked the obsidian water below.

The pilot veered left, and I kept firing. One of my bullets angled through the door and tagged the pilot in the head.

Blood splattered against the glass, and the helicopter soon spiraled. The tail whipped around, and the craft plummeted toward the water.

It smacked the surface and tumbled, the rotors snapping as they impacted the swells. The fuselage bobbed on the water for a few moments before sinking into the abyss, water swirling around it.

JD eased up on the throttle but still kept us barreling back toward Coconut Key.

"Is everybody okay?" he shouted over the engines.

I gave a glance to Lily, and she nodded. Her heart pounded so hard, her body visibly shook.

We all took a moment to catch our breath as we bounced across the water, the moon and stars amused.

"Let me take a look at that stone," JD said. "I want to see what we just risked our lives for."

I moved forward, took a seat in one of the helm chairs, and pulled the gem from my wetsuit pocket. I handed it to JD, and he studied it carefully. He pulled out a small UV flashlight on his keychain and shined it on the stone.

My whole body tensed.

## 52

I  t didn't glow.

Rubies glow under UV light. It must have been garnet or red topaz.

Whatever it was, it wasn't the Jewel of Aphrodite.

My jaw tightened, and Lily's eyes rounded. Her jaw went slack as she stared at the fake gem in disbelief.

My glare turned to her. "Where's the real ruby?"

She was speechless for a moment. She shook her head, and her raven hair fluttered in the breeze. "I don't know."

My accusatory gaze blazed into her.

"Don't look at me. I didn't have time to switch the stone."

"Maybe you did?"

She tucked her chin, incredulous. "When?"

"You had a few minutes in the tender by yourself."

"A few minutes with Anatoly's goons shooting at me. Then I circled around and picked your ass up. Or have you forgotten that already?"

My doubtful gaze persisted.

"What do you want to do? Strip-search me?"

JD's eyes brightened. "It's the only way to be sure."

She sneered at him.

Lily had a few places to hide a gem. I patted her down and searched the wetsuit's zippered pouches, coming up empty-handed.

"Satisfied?"

"Not really."

"You want me to strip, squat, and cough?"

I just stared at her.

"I didn't swap the stones. Has it occurred to you that maybe Le Grand tried to screw Anatoly and switched the jewel? Maybe Anatoly knew it was junk."

"Why did he chase after us if he knew? Surely he would have evaluated the stone during the exchange."

I continued to stare at Lily with suspicious eyes. She could have swallowed the damn thing, though I don't think it would have been too much fun coming out the other end.

There was one other place it could be.

"Fine," she said in an exasperated breath. Her fingers tugged the zipper of her wetsuit, and she peeled out of the neoprene. Her buoyant peaks bounced, and the moonlight glowed her skin.

"It's nothing I haven't seen already," I said.

JD tried not to look. He didn't try very hard.

Lily stepped close, grabbed my hand, and placed it on her smooth peach. She could have copped a squat and coughed, but I think she wanted to make things more interesting. I felt around, strictly for professional reasons.

She squirmed slightly as I probed her warm center. Her sultry eyes gazed at me, her pupils wide. "Happy?"

"Well, it's not up there."

"Maybe I should let you strip search me more often."

"You two need to get a room."

"Tyson doesn't trust me anymore," Lily said.

"I never did."

"How do you expect a relationship to work without trust?"

"Leaving me on the boat wasn't the best way to build trust."

"I came back," she said with an innocent shrug.

She left the wetsuit on the deck and put on dry clothes.

Her eyes rounded with a sudden realization. "Annabelle. That fucking bitch. She switched the stones when Anatoly showed her the ruby in the forward lounge."

The moment flashed before my eyes. Anatoly had handed her the jewel. Annabelle looked at it briefly, then gave him a hug and a kiss, switching the stone behind his back. When she pulled away, she handed him the fake, which he then put into the safe.

It all made sense.

JD angled the boat around, and we headed back toward Cuban waters.

Lily texted Annabelle from her sat phone. [Are you okay? Just checking on you.]

There was no response.

We raced back to the superyacht.

It came into view after a few minutes. The speck on the horizon grew larger.

Deckhands buzzed about, trying to figure out what the hell to do with the dead bodies. I had no doubt the Cuban authorities had been notified and were on their way. We had to get in and get out quickly.

As we drew within range of the superyacht, another Go Fast boat pulled to the stern. It was white with red trim. The 5 outboard engines burbled.

Annabelle hustled down the steps, a small clutch dangling from her shoulder. She boarded the boat from the swim platform. The driver throttled up, and the engines spit a rooster tail as it took off. The boat skipped across the inky swells, and JD changed course, heading after them.

We skimmed the water, traveling way too fast for this kind of chop. We bounced and smashed the waves. Each time the boat smacked the surface, a jolt ran through my spine.

The boat ahead was fast, but not as fast as the *Apex*, even with only five working engines. We gained on them slowly, following north, heading back toward the Keys.

I hung on for dear life as we crashed through the swells.

My mind swirled with possibilities, thinking about everything that had transpired. I gave another accusatory glance to Lily. "This was all part of the plan, wasn't it?"

She looked at me, dumbfounded. "What are you talking about?"

"That's why you needed our help. This was all a decoy so your accomplice could get away with the gem."

Her eyes rounded, and her jaw dropped. "No. It wasn't part of the plan. Trust me, I feel just as screwed over as you do."

"Somehow, I don't think so."

"I'm telling you the truth."

I stared deep into her eyes, searching for the truth. She didn't blink or look away.

We kept after Annabelle.

As we drew near the Go Fast boat, more gunfire erupted. Bullets zipped across the water. A few of them pelted the front windshield, webbing it with cracks.

We ducked for cover, and JD kept on the throttle.

At this point, we were running low on ammunition.

More bullets sprayed across the bow as JD veered toward the port side of the Go Fast boat. There were three people aboard the boat, including Annabelle.

I crouched below the starboard gunwale, angling my rifle at the goon shooting at us. He was at the stern, firing over the outboards. It was almost impossible to keep an accurate sight picture. I tried to time the peaks and valleys. I held my breath and waited for the right moment.

## 53

I squeezed the trigger a few times, and bullets rocketed across the water. Hot brass ejected from the port, tumbling over the gunwale. My bullets hit the water, just shy of the stern, sending plumes of mist into the air.

I readjusted and continued to fire amid the swells while bullets snapped overhead.

Lily fired alongside me.

We kept firing as the chase continued. I tried to conserve my ammo, but I ran through my last magazine in no time. The bolt locked forward. Empty.

I tossed the AR aside and drew my pistol.

Lily continued to squeeze off rounds and tagged the shooter in the throat. I'm not sure if it was luck or skill. Blood spewed from his carotid artery as the thug tumbled back to the deck. It was a nasty place to take a bullet. His throat looked like ground beef.

Annabelle screamed, though the roar of the engines obscured it.

We kept gaining on the boat, and eventually, JD pulled alongside.

The driver drew a pistol and fired a couple shots in our general direction.

Another bullet smacked into the glass windshield, leaving another hole.

I returned fire.

We were close enough now to be relatively accurate. I put a couple rounds into the guy. He flopped against the wheel, and blood splattered the console.

Annabelle shrieked again and pushed him aside. She took over and veered starboard, pulling away from us.

JD followed, and soon we were alongside her again.

She throttled up and tried to pull away.

It was a game of chicken at this point. How fast were you willing to go, given the worsening conditions?

The waves grew higher as the impending storm pushed closer.

The boats bounced and rolled on the chop.

I don't think Annabelle had a lot of experience at the helm of this kind of vessel. She bounced across the swells, and the nose caught air. It lifted like a 747 on the runway. The boat launched toward the sky on a draft. It went vertical, hung in the air for a moment, then looped upside down and smacked against the water. Bits of fiberglass broke off, and the capsized boat rose and fell on the swells.

JD backed off the throttle and circled around the wreckage.

There wasn't any sign of Annabelle.

I dove into the water and swam to the wreckage. I pulled myself underneath the boat and searched the dark water for Annabelle.

I didn't see her anywhere.

The running lights for the boat were still on, and interior lighting glowed the water. There was a small capsule of air inside the passenger compartment of the capsized boat. I swam up and grabbed a breath as it rolled on the swells. I looked around and saw her small leather clutch floating in the water. I grabbed it, and something rattled inside.

I unclasped the latch and looked in.

The ruby was captivating.

I snapped the latch shut before it had a chance to spill out and plummet to the depths below. The seal was tight, trapping air in the small purse.

I dove down and pulled myself under the gunwale, then swam to the surface and grabbed a breath of air.

JD and Lily watched from the *Apex*.

I swam to the stern and climbed aboard at the swim platform.

"Nice purse," Lily joked as I entered the aft lounge, dripping wet.

"It's a very nice purse." I opened it and pulled out the gem.

Lily's eyes rounded.

The Jewel of Aphrodite sparkled in the moonlight.

JD fished out his UV flashlight and shined it on the stone.

It glowed.

We all grinned, admiring the real jewel.

I slipped it into the zippered pocket in my wetsuit and sealed it. I wasn't letting the damn thing out of my sight.

JD took the helm, and we circled around the wreckage a few times, looking for Annabelle.

We never found her.

The seas continued to get rougher.

JD throttled up and headed north, leaving the mangled boat behind. We managed to keep ahead of the storm. The ride was a little bumpy, but I tried to relax.

"Where does this leave us?" Lily asked.

"What do you mean?" I knew what she meant.

"I told you we'd get the jewel back. I guess we're even now."

"Well, if you hadn't stolen it in the first place…"

She rolled her eyes. "Like I said, it's in my nature."

"I think you have two sides."

"We all do, don't we?"

There was a little good and bad in all of us. A little yin and yang. Every day has its night. The battle of two wolves. Which one do you feed?

We weren't too far from Coconut Key when the thump of rotor blades filled the air. It could only mean one thing.

I grabbed the rocket launcher and casually slipped it into the water. It wasn't registered, and we didn't have a tax stamp. Not exactly legal.

Soon the bluish glow of a spotlight shined down on us from above. A UH-60 Coast Guard helicopter hovered overhead. A voice addressed us through a speaker above and told us to heave to and prepare to be boarded.

Two Coast Guard patrol boats appeared out of the inky blackness and pulled alongside us. A petty officer shouted through a megaphone. "United States Coast Guard. Do you have weapons aboard?"

I flashed my badge and said, "Yes."

The defender class patrol boats pulled along either side. A petty officer tossed me a line, and I tied off on a cleat.

"What are you doing out on the water tonight?"

JD shrugged. "Just a leisurely cruise."

The petty officer surveyed the bullet holes in the hull and the engine cowling.

"Leisurely, huh?"

He boarded the boat with another officer. "Want to tell me about the damage?"

We all exchanged an awkward glance.

"We were pursuing international jewel thieves," I said.

It sounded ridiculous, like something out of a spy movie.

Petty officer Baxter lifted a curious brow, his face full of skepticism. "A little out of your jurisdiction, aren't you?"

"Are we outside of the county?" I asked, playing dumb.

"Well outside," he emphasized. "You're in international waters."

"I didn't realize," I said innocently.

"You boys seem armed to the teeth."

I shrugged. "We've seen an uptick in crime lately."

He looked at me flatly, not amused.

## 54

"Call Sheriff Daniels with Coconut County," I said. "He'll verify anything you need to know."

"Whose boat is this?" Petty Officer Baxter asked.

There was another awkward moment.

"It's mine," Lily said.

"I need to see your license and registration."

She shifted uncomfortably.

JD muttered in my ear, "I guess we're about to find out if the boat is stolen."

"It's not actually my boat," Lily said. "I'm borrowing it from a friend."

"You're borrowing it?" the petty officer repeated with a healthy dose of skepticism.

Lily fumbled for the registration in a compartment at the helm station and gave him her ID.

He looked over the registration, then her ID card. I was sure it was fake.

He radioed in the information to command, and we all waited eagerly.

Lily was as cool as a cucumber. She didn't seem flustered at all.

"So, let me get this straight. You're out here in the middle of the night, chasing jewel thieves with short-barreled AR 15s and a boat full of holes?"

"It's complicated," I said. "And I've got a tax stamp for the gun and the suppressor."

Jack struck up a conversation with Baxter. JD's buddy in the Coast Guard was pretty high up. He suggested the petty officer get in touch. Baxter returned to his patrol boat and made a few calls while the other officers stood on deck, keeping watch.

Baxter returned a while later. The anticipation was nerve-wracking.

The racing boat came back clean. Not stolen. The petty officer had contacted the owner, and he was aware that Lily had the boat. He'd also spoken to the sheriff.

Daniels was not thrilled about our little adventure, but he confirmed our story as best he could. He was going to be pissed that we didn't keep him in the loop.

They still searched the boat and did a routine safety inspection, making sure we had the appropriate number of life preservers, flares, and other regulated items.

"The next time you guys take it upon yourselves to pursue jewel thieves in international waters, contact us so we can provide support."

"You got it," I said.

The petty officers boarded their boat, and we cast off the lines. The spotlight from the helicopter above went out, and the UH-60 peeled away. The patrol boats throttled up and disappeared into the abyss.

Lily smiled.

"Let me see your ID," I said.

She handed it to me.

"Lily Jordan, huh?" I examined it carefully. "This is a nice fake."

"Thank you. I have connections."

"Whose boat is this, really?"

"It's a friend's. I swear."

I left it at that.

JD took the helm, and we cruised back to Coconut Key at a leisurely pace.

It wasn't long before we pulled into the marina at *Diver Down* and tied off in an empty slip. We unloaded the gear, and there was another awkward moment when we finished.

"I guess this is goodbye," Lily said.

"You're not going to stick around?"

"Why? So you can arrest me?"

"I can't be totally sure, but I think you helped me get the jewel back."

Her eyes narrowed at me. "I helped you. It wasn't a diversion to steal the ruby. I swear."

"I guess we'll never know."

"Look into my eyes. Am I lying?"

I surveyed her baby blues for a moment. She didn't blink. She didn't flinch. I'd been around a lot of poker players, and everybody had a tell. But I couldn't spot hers.

"Stay out of trouble," I cautioned.

She smirked. "But trouble is so much fun."

She lifted on her tiptoes and kissed me on the cheek. It was a nice kiss. Warm, tender, heartfelt.

Lily pulled away and stared at me for a long moment. "My friend is going to be so upset about the boat."

I chuckled. "I'm sure you'll charm your way out of it."

"I always do."

We looked at each other for another long moment.

"Goodbye, Lily."

"Goodbye, Tyson."

She climbed into the boat, and I cast off the lines. We watched her idle out of the marina.

"You better make sure she didn't pinch that gem from you," JD commented as we watched her go.

Lily waved one last time as she neared the breakwater.

I felt the zippered pouch in my wetsuit.

The stone was still there.

I unzipped it and decided to get a visual on it just for good measure.

It was safe and sound.

We grabbed the gear and lugged it to the *Avventura*. Buddy greeted us excitedly as we stepped into the salon. We stowed the gear, and JD made his way behind the bar and poured us both a drink. We lifted our glasses to toast.

"Helluva night," he said.

We clinked glasses and sipped the fine whiskey. All was right in the world again.

I called Jean-Claude and arranged to return the stone. He and his bodyguards were at the marina in no time.

I told him we had recovered it from Anatoly. I left Lily out of it. He thanked me profusely and wanted to wire money into my account. I told him to make a donation to a local charity instead, and he agreed.

"Back to the museum now?" I asked.

"Not until they get better security."

Jean-Claude left with his guards, and the jewel was no longer my responsibility.

JD crashed on the boat in his VIP stateroom after we'd put back a few more drinks.

In the morning, the smell of freshly brewed coffee and bacon wafted up to my stateroom. I pulled myself out of bed, got dressed, and stumbled down to the galley where he had prepared a breakfast fit for kings. He had an ear-to-ear grin on his face. "You're not going to believe what I found?"

I shrugged.

He grabbed a paperback from the counter and held it up. It was *20,000 Leagues Under the Sea*—the book where he had written the secret location of the lost treasure of Jacques De La Fontaine.

"Where did you find it?"

"It was in a compartment in my stateroom," he said sheepishly.

I scowled at him. He'd been blaming the missing book on me for months.

"I must have moved it and forgotten."

I tapped my skull and mocked, "Old-timers."

He frowned at me. "I am not *that* old, and my memory works just fine. Perhaps I was a little inebriated when I misplaced it."

"A likely story."

JD dished up the plates, and we ate on the sky deck, taking in the beautiful sunrise. The orange sun bathed the marina in warm light. Gulls hung on the breeze, and boats swayed in their slips.

This was the good life. There was no doubt about it.

We'd been on a lot of adventures together, and there were

plenty more to come. We still had a shipwreck to salvage. Spring Break was right around the corner, and the island was always deluged with partygoers. Some pretty heinous things happened last year, and I hoped the action would stay relatively tame this time around.

We weren't but a few days into the bikini season when Daniels called with our next adventure.

*Ready for more?*

*The adventure continues with Wild Greed!*

*Join my newsletter and find out what happens next!*

# AUTHOR'S NOTE

Thanks for all the great reviews!

I've got more adventures for Tyson and JD. Stay tuned.

If you liked this book, let me know with a review on Amazon.

Thanks for reading!

*—Tripp*